Giggs

DR. MELVIN J. BAGLEY

Giggs

FIVE SHADES OF BLUE

DO YOU HAVE
A DATE
FOR PROM?

Please meet in front of the library after school tomorrow night.

TATE PUBLISHING
AND ENTERPRISES, LLC

Published by Tate Publishing & Enterprises, LLC
127 E. Trade Center Terrace | Mustang, Oklahoma 73064 USA
1.888.361.9473 | www.tatepublishing.com

Tate Publishing is committed to excellence in the publishing industry. The company reflects the philosophy established by the founders, based on Psalm 68:11,
"The Lord gave the word and great was the company of those who published it."

Book design copyright © 2015 by Tate Publishing, LLC. All rights reserved.
Cover design by Joana Quilantang
Interior design by Mary Jean Archival

Published in the United States of America

ISBN: 978-1-68028-784-4
Fiction / Romance / General
15.01.14

To my loving daughters Nancy McGuire, Mari Bochanis, Hawley Doyle, and Bobbi Hendricks, who were always by my side.

Contents

Giggs's Plan

It was March 1940 at Granite High School, located at 33 Block South Salt Lake City, a little farming community on the outskirts of the city. Being an agricultural community, the school took the Fighting Farmers as a mascot. On the back of their football stadium was painted a twelve-foot farmer who stood tall and proud, pitchfork in hand and a single piece of straw resting in between his curled lips. Gerald Bagley was a senior that year and just two months from his high school graduation. Everyone called him Giggs, but not a single person could tell you where he got the nickname, not even Gerald himself. Giggs was dating a girl named Barbara Beasley, who was shaped like an hourglass and was really out of Gigg's league where looks were concerned. Her nickname was "The Weasel" because she was a professional at weaseling her way out of anything and everything that she didn't feel like doing. Giggs and the Weasel had been going steady for nearly six months by the time March rolled around, so he naturally assumed that his prom date that year was taken care of. You know what they say about assuming, though.

"So what do you want to do prom night?" Giggs asked Barbara as they strolled down the hallway between classes.

"What do you mean?" she asked, whipping her auburn hair around so that it splashed over smooth, ivory shoulders.

"Well, aren't we going to prom together?" he asked, his brow wrinkled the way it always did when he was confused.

"Actually, Vaughn Benion asked me to go," she said, her blue eyes dropping to the black and white linoleum floor.

"The star of the basketball team?" Giggs blurted incredulously, mouth agape.

"Why do you look so surprised?" Barbara asked defensively, slamming a pale hand down on her hip.

"No, it's not that. It's just...I thought we would go... together..."

"I know, I'm sorry, Giggs, really, I am. But he did ask first, and it is *Vaughn*..."

"No, I get it," he said with a hangdog expression. "I should've asked sooner."

Giggs was a little hurt by the news, but he couldn't blame the Weasel for wanting to go with a big shot like Vaughn. He was a big deal all over school. Granite High basketball was famous for being the best. The team had just won its fifth straight state championship, and Vaughn was the face of the team—he had been since he was just a sophomore.

Gerald Bagley, on the other hand, was never the most popular guy. He was a little scrawny and had never quite grown into his enormous size-thirteen feet. He wore his pants just a little too short and he was never seen anywhere without his heavy black-framed glasses that constantly slid down his sharp nose. Whether it was a blessing or a curse, no one could say, but Giggs seemed to be the only person in school who didn't realize his place in the social pecking order, and that gave him a special kind of confidence he wore like a badge. That is how he landed the Weasel in the first place. He was just too naïve to realize he was out of his league. His self-assurance must have taken her so off guard that she just went along with it when he asked her to go steady.

Once his own girlfriend shot him down, Giggs knew that his time was limited to snatch up a date for the last dance of his high school career. When he couldn't think of a single girl other than Barbara he wanted to take, he decided to do something a little out of the ordinary. The next day Giggs ran an ad in *The Granician*, the high school paper, which read:

> If you don't have a date for the Senior Prom and are
> someone who would like to go, please meet in front of
> the library after school tomorrow night.

Now, this was a bold move on Giggs's part—one because there was a good chance that no one was going to show, and two because there was as good of a chance that someone *would* answer the ad, but it wouldn't be anyone he would want to take. He considered both of those options before dropping off his little note and the 25 cents it cost to put an ad in the school paper and decided that it didn't matter who it was who showed, he'd just be happy to have a date.

Every girl deserves a Senior Prom, he thought as he slipped out of the school newspaper room. *Whoever it is who shows, I'll make sure she has a night to remember.*

That day after the last bell rang, Giggs took his time getting to the library so he wouldn't seem too desperate. When he finally strolled in as cool and collected as he could, he was shocked to see that there was not one, but five senior girls there in response to his ad—Rosela McMillan-Baldwin, Jean Whitehead, Faye Briner, Beverly Butterworth, and Lois Wright. None of these girls were terribly popular in school, which is probably why they did not have dates to the prom.

They were a small union of misfits, each with her own special quirk. Giggs took a look at each of them. There was one girl much taller than him who looked red-faced and sweaty like she'd just run a marathon—he thought he recognized her from the golf course that he caddied at from time to time. Another girl there looked to have a severe snaggletooth. Giggs noticed it during her spilt-second smile just before her hand shot up to cover her mouth. There was also a young lady who must have been two times his weight, and two who just seemed to be scared of their own shadows, their body language letting him know they might flee at any moment.

Once his initial observations were complete, he said, "Hello, ladies. My name is Gerald Bagley, but you can call me Giggs. So, would you ladies be interested in going to the Senior Prom?" He rocked back and fourth in his polished Oxfords, his voice shaking just a little.

"All of us?" the girl named Faye asked, who seemed to be the most assertive of the introverted bunch.

"All of you," he said as he nodded. "We'll go not just as a couple, but as five girls and a guy."

A couple of the girls blinked hard at the response Giggs gave, one cocked her head and stared, and the others just sat quietly and mulled it over. The request on first hearing it seemed absolutely crazy, but Giggs went on to explain his plan to the girls.

"You all don't have a date, and neither do I. If I take you all, we can all at least get into the prom and have a chance at a good time. I'll take all five of you and make sure you're night is something special—at least more special than sitting at home on your rumps. Some of the most popular boys will be there, you know? Who's to say they won't come over and dance with you? And I will make sure that all of you get to dance. You have my word on that."

"Sounds a little nutso, Giggs," Faye said.

Dr. Melvin J. Bagley

Beverly nodded, and the other three nodded as well to show they all thought this was a crazy scheme Giggs had cooked up.

"What have we got to lose?" Giggs asked, shrugging his shoulders.

Although the girls thought it sounded a little bit strange, they thought about what Giggs said and realized he may have had a point. They came to the conclusion that even if they all had to share a date, they would at least get a chance to go.

"So it's unanimous," Faye said. "I guess will be a sextuplet then."

"It's a date!" He smiled. "Or it's five dates," he corrected himself with a wink.

After that, Giggs took all the money he had made as a caddy at the Salt Lake Country Club and rented a limousine to take his dates to prom in. While Giggs got all the details worked out with the car, a tuxedo, and the schedule, each of the girls set off to find the perfect gown. It was the first dance any of them had been invited to, so Rosela, Beverly, Faye, Jeanne, and Lois were all in a dream state as they sifted through dress racks at the department stores, thrift stores, family closets, and consignment shops to find something perfect.

When the big night rolled around, he picked the girls up, one by one, at each of their houses. Each girl was dressed to the hilt in long, flowing gowns with hairs pinned and curled. It was the first time a couple of them had ever even worn rouge or lipstick. He pinned on their corsages, told each girl how beautiful she was, and off they went to the Granite High gym where the Senior Prom was held.

"I feel like a movie star," Jeanne blushed as she slid in beside Beverly.

"I know," Beverly gushed. "I've never been in a limousine."

The six Granite High seniors arrived to their ball and walked inside together. There were flowers and candles all over the gymnasium, and tables set out with ironed white linen tablecloths draped over them with honeycomb pattern vases stuffed full of pale yellow roses in the middle. A band played at one end of the gym, as the six worked their way to a table nearby the men who were crooning into microphones. Griggs pulled out the chair for each of his dates and then took a seat himself.

"May I have this dance?" Griggs said to Rosela. She nodded and Griggs swept her out onto the floor. Next he danced with Lois, then Beverly, then Faye, but when he got to Jeanne she insisted that she would rather just sit and talk to the other girls.

"Just one dance," Griggs insisted. "And I won't ask again."

"Okay, one," Jeanne acquiesced. "But only one."

"That's all I ask," Griggs promised.

Most of the girls were also asked by another boy, some two, to dance as well. It turned out to be a night that changed each of their lives forever, but none of them would know what kind of effect it had on the others until forty years later, when they all met again for the first time since they graduated high school.

Years went by and their fortieth high school reunion rolled around. They were not able to talk at the reunion, but just before they all parted ways Beverly gathered everyone that had been at prom that night and suggested, "Hey, what do you all say we all meet again, just the five of us, this fall? Let's say…" She pulled a small calendar from her purse and said, "On October 1, just to share what all has happened with us. I don't know about you all, but I'd like to catch up with everyone. Plus I know that I would like to thank Giggs for inviting us to the prom!"

"I love it!" Rosela agreed. "My whole life changed because of that night. It's just too much to tell right here. I'll be there!"

The other three women agreed they would be there as well.

"Now all we have to do is get a hold of Giggs," Beverly said. "Just leave that to me."

Beverly did indeed get a hold of Giggs, who had already left the reunion that night, and on October 1, 1980, four of the five women and Giggs met at the Jeremy Ranch Country Club. Jeanne was the only one missing, which was a disappointment to the little group. Everybody was looking forward to catching up with long lost friends, and they each wondered if the next had a story just as shocking as their own to tell.

"Well, I guess we might as well take a seat," Rosela said, her eyes trained on the front door, hoping she'd see Jeanne walk in.

"I guess so," said Faye. "It's just a shame that—"

"Well, look there!" Beverly interrupted, and the table turned to see what it was Beverly was smiling about. It was Jeanne Whitehead, standing at the host station and scanning the room in search for her old prom dates.

2

Jeanne Whitehead

The Dance

"Jeanne, Jeanne! We're over here!" Rosela, Beverly, and Faye all shouted across the hushed country club dining room in unison. Jeanne blushed as she hurried over to them, passing stuffy men and women in polo shirts and loafers and tennis skirts whose eyes she could feel burrowing into her.

"Well, you all are quite the welcoming committee," she said in almost a whisper as she greeted her overly enthusiastic friends.

"You came!" Faye gushed. "Yay, Jeanne, you came!"

They all hugged and laughed, and a couple of the more sentimental members of the little group shed a few tears. As each of the women and Giggs gave Jeanne a hug, she felt moved by their overt display of friendly affection, but at the same time she felt a knot that had formed earlier that day in her stomach tighten.

What are they going to think of me? she wondered as she took her seat at the linen covered table.

"You look fantastic, Jeanne," Beverly said once they were all settled back into their seats. "You're as fit as you always were."

Jeanne was, in fact, very fit. She had always had an athletic build from her years playing basketball and golf and running track. Even in a pair of slacks, a simple button-down blouse, and a pair of flats, you could see that she had a nice figure.

"I try," she said as she wiped away the beads of sweat that had formed on the water glass in front of her folded napkin.

"You've never had to try," Lois smiled. "You're just one of those blessed people."

"So, Jeanne, what in the world have you been up to?" Faye chimed in. "Please, please tell us everything."

As Jeanne looked around the table at the smiling faces that surrounded her, she thought about how glad she was that she had decided to go to the get-together. When the idea to meet in a scaled down setting after the reunion was first presented, she felt torn about attending. On one hand, she yearned to get the opportunity to sit down and get reconnected with high school friends. But there was also a part of her that dreaded the intimate setting, and the idea of sharing everything about herself with people she had not seen in years. For weeks she wavered on whether or not to really go, but the more she vacillated over it, the more she talked herself into it. *I'll be fifty-eight soon*, she thought. *Why shouldn't I go?*

"Well," Jeanne said. "Let's see. Where shall I begin? It's been a while."

"Begin at the beginning," Faye chirped. "We want to hear it all!"

The other four women had kept in touch somewhat over the years. They had exchanged Christmas cards, and some knew children's and even grandchildren's names. Jeanne was the only one who seemed to have fallen off the map completely, so they were chomping at the bit to hear what she had been doing the last forty years.

"Well, I went to University of Utah and got my bachelor's and then my master's, both in business," she said. "And I just lucked into the job I have now. I'm a stenographer."

"That's an interesting career." Giggs said.

"Well, what else?" Beverly boomed, but before she could answer the table erupted into chatter.

"Who wants a mimosa?" Beverly asked as she waved down a server.

"None for me," Faye said. "I'll stick with my water."

"Well, I'll have hers then," Rosela joked.

Jeanne sat quietly, being the most reserved of the bunch, and listened as the four women and Giggs broke off in pairs and talked crazily as if each were trying to out-talk the other. As the table buzzed with the scrambled chatter of five other voices talking and laughing, Jeanne thought about Beverly's question, "What else?" What all had she done since that night that brought them all together?

❦

"Not so tight!" Jeanne whined. She was tired of all this primping, plucking, and polishing, just for another tired, old church dance. Her older sister, Jeri, was tightening her corset and Jeanne swore that she must have been trying to break her ribs.

"I thought these things were extinct," she moaned.

"I found this in the attic," Jeri said firmly and she knitted her brow and pulled tightly on the corset strings. "It was with a bunch of other old clothes of Grandma's. It really has a marvelous slimming effect on you, Jeanne. The guys are going to be drooling."

"Great." Jeanne rolled her eyes.

"I don't know why you are even going to this thing, the way you complain about dances," Jeri said, shaking her head and studying her little sister.

"You know that mom all but makes me," Jeanne said. "Plus, as much as I hate dresses and dances, I like to see the elders and make them happy. I think they get a kick out of these things…I don't know why, though."

Jeanne really did hate primping, and she also despised the weekly Saturday night dances her church put on in the cultural hall. She didn't just find them boring, she described the dances as "excruciating" and even "humiliating."

"Girls just stand there while all these really 'swell' guys gawk at them," she complained, adding a sarcastic emphasis on *swell*. "They all look at you like a piece of meat! And on top of it, we have to get a special card signed by the bishop before we can even attend!"

"Is it really such a horror, Jeanne?"

"Psh!" she scoffed. "Go in and get an interview and then see if you pass go! Really, how humiliating!"

"I swear, Jeanne. You really are impossible," Jeri sighed. "But that is why we love you so." Her lips broke into a faint smile.

While Jeanne loathed the dances that her church put on, she was born and raised in a strong Latter Day Saint family, and family and faith were the focal point of her upbringing, with her love of sports ranking a close second in her life.

"Jeanne, Jeri, are you ready yet?" her mother called from the bottom of the basement stairs.

They lived in an old Victorian house with a massive basement that you could get to from the kitchen. The large, musty home was built during the early years of Salt Lake City's beginnings. Almost all the houses from the era had the same kinds of basements for families who practiced food storage, which was encouraged by the LDS church leaders to prepare for any unforeseeable hard times. Barbara, Jeanne's mother, had been in the basement organizing bins and jars of fruit that she had put up over the summer. She took everything the elders said very seriously, and so the family's basement tended to resemble a small grocery store.

Canning goods and preparing for whatever cataclysmic event the Church of the Latter Day Saints feared was a family affair. Barbara and the two girls bottled raspberries, peaches, cherries, and pears that Jeanne's two younger brothers helped their father harvest. It was a huge undertaking, but the family always agreed it was worth it when the cold winter months lingered in Utah like a nagging chest cold and no fruit was available in the markets.

"We'll be down in a minute, Mom," Jeri called back.

"Are Allen or Heller coming?" Jeanne asked.

Allen and Heller were Jeanne's two brothers who were dance-age appropriate, fourteen and fifteen, respectively. It was a standard routine for the boys to accompany Jeri and Jeanne when they went to any dances. Jeanne liked that her kid brothers tagged along because they were much more willing to get into mischief with her on the way. The only highlight to the dreadful events, according to Jeanne, was the short walk to the chapel, which usually turned into a drawn-out adventure for them. One of Jeanne's favorite things to do as they strolled to the despised dances was to swipe a few of the apples off of their neighbor's tree and see who could hold the most fruit under their shirts without calling attention to themselves. Jeri would never participate in any of these antics. She was the serious, studious one. Being the oldest of the children, she felt it was her job to set an example for her younger siblings. She sang in the church choir, played the piano, got straight A's, and never, ever uttered a cuss word!

Stealing apples and shoving them down her blouse was hardly her cup of tea.

Jeri and Jeanne were not only different in their personalities, they were also polar opposites in the looks department. Where Jeanne was tall and somewhat plain, Jeri was stunning—the kind of girl they put on magazine covers. Jeanne had the same color hair as her older sister, but that was the only feature they shared. The younger sister was tall and awkward, with a muscular build. She had hard curves in her face and never entertained the idea of applying makeup or curling her hair to soften them. That night, however, she was as dolled up as she had ever been. She wore her self-consciousness as plainly as her rouge. She was much more comfortable in denim and a ponytail.

Jeri had ivory skin, high cheekbones, and long brunette hair that shone like maple syrup in the light. She had enormous chocolate-colored eyes that sloped just slightly down at the edges and framed by her long, thick eyelashes.

"Her eyelashes were the longest the pediatrician had ever seen," Barbara always told people. "She was the most beautiful baby I'd ever laid eyes on."

She was a natural beauty and really didn't need to wear any rouge or face powder to look like she'd walked right off a *Look* magazine cover, but when she did apply a dab of each she was a sight to behold. Jeanne couldn't go anywhere with her sister without noticing every male's head snap around for a double as they passed. Whistles, smiles, and flirtatious gestures would abound, but Jeri was much too staid to return the favor.

Jeri was more than just gorgeous, she was confident, intelligent, and had an incredible personality. Jeanne loved her older sister dearly, and never found herself jealous of her sister's beauty or the attention she got from the less fair sex. It all actually intrigued Jeanne in a way. How could someone so beautiful and kind be so smart too? Weren't the gals with the looks supposed to be kind of dimwitted? If that were true, then Jeri broke the mold, and she loved that about her sister. Jeanne couldn't have been more proud of Jeri.

"Who's running the records tonight?" Heller asked Allen as the boys yanked apples off the neighbor's tree. "I heard it was Brother Barlow and he's supposed to play some real swift songs."

"You not playing, Jeanne?" Allen asked, turning to his sister as he crammed apples down his shirt.

"Corset," she groaned, patting at her rigid waistline.

When they finally made it to the hall, every set of eyes attached to a boy's face landed on Jeri as they entered. Jeanne was a spectator of this little game and loved to watch the expressions on all the boys' faces when her sister walked into a room. She was so busy observing that she never noticed if anyone was giving her the "eye."

Jeanne had more important things on her mind to bother with than boys. She was a dedicated basketball player, and as natural as her sister was at calculus and looking beautiful,

Jeanne was the same at shooting three-pointers. She was nearly six feet tall, her height she inherited from her 6'4" father. He had also attended Granite High and played varsity basketball, lettering all four years. Jeanne, too, lettered from the time she was a freshman. She was also the captain of the girls' track team, pole vaulting up to ten feet. She held the county record and would most likely be attending college on a track scholarship.

As much as she protested the dance, Jeanne ended up having a great night with Jeri and her brothers. She danced with the buddy of whoever had asked Jeri to dance, so she always had a partner. Her favorite dance partner was a boy in her chemistry class named Spencer Hutchings. Spencer was the only boy tall enough to twirl the long-limbed Jeanne.

She didn't know it that night when Spencer spun her around the dance floor, but he had had a secret crush on her since they were fourteen. He was a kind, gentle, soft-spoken boy, so the thought of telling her was almost more than he could bear. Only once did he try to kiss her, and that was just because she told him he could. It was just on the cheek, but he did even that awkwardly. That night he must have been feeling bold because in the middle of a slow song he blurted, "Jeanne, will you wear my class ring?"

Great! What have I done! she thought as she fumbled for something to say.

"Oh, I don't think I should," she finally spit out. "I mean, I'd have to talk to my parents and all that."

A few dances, a little bitty peck on the cheek, and he was all but making wedding plans. *Good grief*, Jeanne thought. *I had no idea boys were so sappy and sentimental!*

The Ring

Summer whirled by in a glorious fury of swimming pools, camping trips, golf, and nonstop basketball, but fall was fast approaching. Jeanne lamented the loss of that magnificent summer. It was the first that her parents had allowed her a little freedom. She was nearly a senior in high school, after all. She got a part-time job at the country club doing odd jobs. Every night that she came home from work that summer, she'd tell a new story about something fantastic she'd discovered at her place of employment.

"The food there is like nothing you've ever seen!" she told her brothers. "I mean, it looks like it should be a centerpiece rather than a meal! And oh boy does it smell like heaven."

The best part of all, though, was the free golf. Every evening after her shift was over she would go out on the driving range and hit golf balls. Like every other sport she tried, she took to golf like a duck to water. By the second day she had the resident golf pros surrounding her, giving her tips and gawking at how natural she was on the green.

"You sure you haven't been doing this for years?" one of the retired pros joked.

"No, sir," Jeanne said. "But I plan on doing it for years to come!"

She learned technique from watching the other women play as the golf pros instructed them. She ended up buying a cheap little set of clubs herself and started playing in the backyard, or anywhere she could. As her golf game improved, she thought about what a pity it was that women didn't really play golf, in competition, anyway. Her high school didn't have a women's golf team.

With her new job and her new fascination with golf, Jeanne didn't have much time for anything else that summer, really. She squeezed in church activities, but found herself dreaming of golf every time she was at a dance or a church raffle. The church functions were the only time she ever saw Spencer, who was taking their relationship much more seriously than Jeanne was. He would drop subtle hints to her about going on a real date or spending more time together, but Jeanne's mind was too focused on golf and her new job to even notice.

When school started, Spencer found himself downtrodden that he and Jeanne would not be in any classes together.

"What's the big deal?" Jeanne asked as he sulked on their walk home.

"I was just hoping to get to see you more than at church stuff," he said.

"You see me after school sometimes," she replied.

"Yeah, I guess," he sighed.

Other girls just didn't appeal to him like Jeanne did. She had spunk, confidence, knew all about sports, and boy could she dance! She was all Spencer could think of. He even contemplated trying out for the track team to try to see her more, but it interfered with basketball so he couldn't.

It was their senior year that year and his primary goal was to get Jeanne to wear his class ring before he left on his church mission. He even tried talking to his dad about it, but his dad reminded him he had more important things to do before he could think about getting serious with a girl— namely his two-year mission overseas. Still, that did not deter him. He asked Jeanne to prom the very next day.

The Perfect Excuse

"Mom, I have a *huge* problem!" Jeanne blurted as she burst through the back door into the kitchen.

"What on earth are you talking about, Jeanne?"

"Oh, Mom, Spencer Hutchings has asked me to the Senior Prom."

"Why, Jeanne Marie Whitehead, what do you mean? All girls want to go to their prom."

Jeanne was nearly in tears as she pleaded with her mother to help fix her strange problem. Her mother could not figure out why a nice boy asking her to prom had upset her so badly. She could see that Jeanne was distressed by the whole ordeal, however, so she offered the only advice she could think of for a problem that didn't seem like a problem at all.

"Just tell Spencer as soon as you can so he can find another date."

"But how?" Jeanne asked as she buried her face in her hands.

"That part is your job," her mother told her as she rubbed her forearm.

Jeanne imagined telling Spencer she couldn't go with him would be one of the hardest, if not the hardest, things she had ever done in her life. It would be more difficult than telling her dad about the time she accidentally spilled a can of paint all over the garage floor, harder than when she told her sister that she had ruined her favorite blouse, even harder than when she had to tell her little brothers that the family dog was missing.

She lay there on the hammock that was tied under a cherry tree in the backyard and pondered over all the different ways to tell Spencer she did not want to go with him. As she fretted over how to break the news, she thoughtlessly flipped through the pages of the high school periodical, *The Granician*. Her eyes floated across the pages when something caught her attention. Lo and behold, the Lord had answered her prayers! There in the top right-hand corner of the page was a wanted ad for girls who didn't yet have a date for prom. It was perfect!

"I've got it!" she exclaimed as she nearly tossed herself out of the hammock. "This is the perfect excuse!"

The next day when she saw Spencer at school, Jeanne unloaded her little white lie.

"I would love to go, Spencer, really, I would, but I can't because I am not allowed to go alone with you. It's my parents. They only allow me to go on group dates. That's why my brothers and sister are always at the dances too."

"Group dates?" he asked, perplexed.

"I know it's strange. But they are my parents so I can't really dispute it too much."

"I guess not," Spencer said with a sigh of defeat.

Now she would have to go through with the second part of her plan, which she thought might be harder than the first. She was going to have to go to the library to meet this Gerald Bagley and see how many other girls responded to the ad. She wasn't quite sure who this Gerald Bagley boy was, but whoever he was, he had just gotten her out of a big pickle. *Thanks, Gerald Bagley!* she thought as she headed to her next class.

When school ended that day, Jeanne stopped to shoot some hoops to ease her nerves and then made her way to the library, where two other girls waited. Not long after she arrived, two more filtered in. Jeanne was a little surprised that five people had responded. She didn't really know any of them well, as none of them played sports. When Gerald himself showed and announced, "My name is Gerald Bagley, but you can call me Giggs," with his polished shoes and his pants that hit right above the ankle, she actually felt relieved at the sight of the gangly teen.

When she went home and announced to her parents that she would not be going with Spencer, but *would* be attending the prom, both her mother and her father sat with dazed looks on their faces.

"So who are you going with? You have to have a date, Jeanne," her mom said.

"With a boy named Gerald."

"Who?" her dad asked.

"Gerald Bagley. Him and four other girls."

"Now what's that?" her dad asked, sitting up in his chair and leaning in toward Jeanne.

"I read about it in the school newspaper Dad, and it sounds perfect for me."

"But why?" her mother asked.

Jeanne exasperated herself explaining why this would be a better choice for her than going with Spencer. She pulled out everything she could think of, until everyone was too confused or too exhausted to ask anymore questions.

"I don't think I'll really ever understand, Jeanne, but you can make your own decisions and I'll stand by whatever you choose," her dad finally said.

"Thank you, Daddy," she said with a smile. As Jeanne walked away, *Granician* in hand, she smiled thinking about how great her dad was.

While her father may have accepted Jeanne's decision without debate, her mother, brothers, and sister could not understand at all why she chose going to the prom with a complete stranger who had four other dates over Spencer. They were completely baffled by her behavior, but after their many attempts at prodding the reason from her failed, they simply gave up. It was an exercise in futility. Neither their inquiries nor their jokes penetrated her, so finally they just gave in and stopped trying to understand their quirky sister.

"I'll let you borrow the dress I wore in the Pioneer Days parade last summer," Jeri offered when she finally gave up on figuring her sister out and decided she would do best to just help her prepare for her strange prom evening. "Mom can sew a few rows of ruffles and lace onto the bottom so it will be long enough for you. You'll be gorgeous!"

The dress was stunning but had been custom made just for Jeri, so Barbara got to work altering it to fit her much larger framed daughter. By the time she was done, the dress was perfectly fitted to Jeanne, all six feet of her. And it even accentuated her tone body, which Jeanne felt a bit uncomfortable about, but also kind of enjoyed.

Prom Night with the Gang

Jeanne was the last girl on Gigg's prom route. When the limousine pulled up in front of the Whitehead's Victorian home, the entire family came out to look inside.

"I feel like a movie star," Jeanne said as she took her seat in the car.

"You look like one." Gerald smiled, tugging at the lapel of his black tuxedo.

"Why, thank you," Jeanne said. "You look swell yourself."

When they got to the gymnasium, the twinkling of candles and smell of fresh cut roses was intoxicating to Jeanne, even though she never cared too much about ornate decorations. The place she usually played basketball in had been transformed to something right out of a movie. The glass vases threw scintilla of candle light across the crisp table cloths as the band was softly playing "Swinging on a Star" by Bing Crosby. As they walked across the slick wood floor, the girls giggled at the attention they were drawing. Gerald strutted in the middle of the five young women like a peacock, so proud of pulling this all together.

They all made it to a table that was close to the band and waited as Gerald scooted each of their seats back for them. They sat for a moment, and when Gerald spotted the first teacher, he felt his self-satisfaction melt into a mushy mess of nerves. Worried that the faculty might frown on his six-some, he quickly grabbed Rosela and began whisking her around the dance floor. Jeanne felt relieved that it wasn't her and turned back to the three remaining girls who were quietly whispering amongst themselves.

Jeanne watched as one boy after the next came to ask one of her cohorts to dance. She had found that avoiding eye contact was the perfect was to divert any unwanted requests. Gerald convinced Jeanne to get up and dance with him, even though she was nearly a head taller, and she realized he was actually quite fun and charming, but that was her only dance of the night.

It went as perfectly as it could go for Jeanne. She had made it to her last prom, got out of going with Spencer and avoided hurting him, and she was able to sit back and relax, and chat with the girls who weren't on the dance floor.

The night flew by and it ended with Rosela, the quietest of the bunch, singing the last song after the singer's voice gave out. The entire table sat in awe as an amazing voice came exploding out of the timid, petite Rosela.

"Why, she has got the most beautiful singing voice I've ever heard," Faye gasped. Jeanne caught a whiff of alcohol as Faye spoke.

"She does," Jeanne agreed, her eyes fixed on Rosela.

When it was finally time to go, the girls and Gerald were exhausted from all the dancing and mingling. It was the most memorable night Jeanne had ever experienced in high school. She had made five new friends, and danced with a boy even though he wasn't tall enough. Quite a night!

Jeanne was humming "Don't Sit under the Apple Tree" as she walked into the house that night. Her mom was up reading a book and could see her glowing from where she sat.

"I guess it went well," she said, laying her book in her lap.

"It did indeed," she said with a smile. They had a quick chat about the night, then off to bed she went.

"I really did have fun tonight," she said before she retired.

As she tiptoed upstairs, she thought about how much she would have missed out on if she would have gone with Spencer. The idea of going with him was neither fun nor exciting, but she found that her stomach fluttered when she thought back over the night.

And all I did was sit and talk to a table of girls I'd never met! she thought. *I guess I just have a different idea of fun.*

The Get-Together

When Jeanne received the reunion invitation in the mail she was ambivalent about going. She hadn't attended any of the previous reunions and did her best to avoid them so she wouldn't wear herself out answering the questions, "Didn't you have children?" and "So you've *never* been married?" She lived a quiet life that she was quite fond of, working as a court stenographer and residing in the "Avenues," a quaint section of Salt Lake City that consisted of mostly professors and other folks who worked at the university. Her cat, Waldo, and her dog, Trinka, were her family. Her parents had both passed, and only her brothers had stayed in Utah. She had a large network of friends from work, but kept mainly to herself. Between her pets and being a member of the Ornithological Society, she kept occupied and was genuinely happy because she was able to be exactly who she was. She knew that she wasn't terribly exciting and couldn't help but fret over what the other girls would think of her life now.

She ended up going to the reunion, and had found a way to dodge the usual grating questions, but then when Beverly suggested they have another get-together, just the six of them, she felt that same soapy bubble of apprehension expand in her stomach. But then she remembered about that night forty years before and what it taught her about herself, and she decided that she should go. She was fifty-eight, after all. She shouldn't care what anyone thought about her or her life.

"So, Jeanne, what else?" Beverly said again over the chatter of the table. "I didn't hear you say that you were married. Why is it you never settled down with a nice man?"

Jeanne paused for a moment as the others at the table waited patiently for her response. She had rehearsed this answer several times in her mind, over and over again. There was never a doubt that this topic was going to come up, her marital status.

"Well, ladies," she started, "Let me try to explain to you. I hope this will not offend any of you, either."

"Go on," Rosela said as all ten eyes at the table were fixed on Jeanne.

"I've led a great life. I have enjoyed good health, a wonderful career, marvelous friends, and a loving family. But I have spent years avoiding the people I knew back in high school for a reason."

"My God, Jeanne, what is it?" Faye exclaimed.

"The reason I turned down my date to the senior prom with Spencer Hutchings is that I never really was attracted to him," she said with slow, deliberate words.

"Well, that's simple enough," Lois said. "He was a plain boy, I guess."

"Well, there's more. He was a great guy, an amazing guy, but the reason I was never attracted to him is because I have never been attracted to any male. I'm gay."

Jeanne watched as a few jaws nearly came unhinged. As she waited for someone to say something, Beverly threw her chair back and shot up out of it like the seat had just bitten her. Jeanne waited for her to leave the room, but what she did was anything but storm out. She headed straight over to Jeanne and wrapped her in her arms.

"Jeanne, we love you!" Beverly exclaimed. "We'll always be your friends. Why in the world didn't you just tell us that? No one cares about your sexual orientation. My goodness!"

"Do you know I thought you wanted to make Spencer jealous?" Faye burst out into laughter. "Funny what the rumor mill churns out!"

Jeanne looked to the others and each person at the table was wearing big smiles. It was the same set of smiles that surrounded her the night she realized why she always felt a little different than other girls. And now she could tell them, after all these years, who she really was. She felt the weight of the world lifted off of her shoulders.

"You know, it's weird, and I don't want you all to think I had the hots for you, but it was the night Giggs took us to prom that I came to terms with who I was. I couldn't figure out a lot of things about me, but that night things just kind of clicked. I think I was terrified to admit it to myself, with my religious upbringing and all that. But the night I sat and talked with the four of you, it hit me. Of course it took a while to come out, but that was my first step." Jeanne paused and grabbed her drink and said, "To Giggs," she said, holding up her glass.

"To Giggs!" the table cried out in unison.

3

Rosela McMilan Baldwin

"Well, I guess I'll go next," Rosela said once everyone had settled from the excitement of the moment. "As you all also know, I too was one of the five ladies fortunate enough, or maybe crazy enough, is more like it," Rosela said with a wink, "to be one of Giggs' prom dates back in 1940. Looking back over my life, I am filled with an overwhelming gratitude for the countless incredible experiences I've had. Listening to Jeanne just made me realize that all those experiences started that one beautiful night in May for me as well. Well," Rosela paused for a second and bit at her top lip, a habit she carried into adulthood from her youth, "I guess it really started one chilly afternoon after school in a musty high school library when I answered the call to this visionary who took me and four other girls to the prom. We thought you were crazy, Giggs." She smiled at Gerald. "But we had an absolute blast and made friendships that have lasted a lifetime."

"That was the intention." Gerald grinned.

"Well, Giggs, ladies," she said, turning to address the table," I don't know that I've ever told any of you, but that night was a jumping off point for me. I mean, really, it was something special. And I want to say thank you, Giggs, for being crazy enough to put it together."

"The pleasure was mine," Gerald assured her.

"Okay, okay," Jeanne piped in. "I don't know that I speak for the table, but the suspense is killing me. Do tell what that night led to, Rosela. The girls may know a bit, but I've been out of the loop so long that I'm dying to hear your story."

Rosela was an only child, raised solely by her father, Dr. Frank Baldwin, a general physician. Dr. Baldwin worked round the clock it seemed, and so he hired a nanny by the name of Bessie Smith to help around the house and play the role of surrogate mother to his only daughter. Bessie was a short, stout woman in her early thirties with heavy laugh lines and dark, wiry hair that never seemed in place. She had a daughter, Regina, who was Rosela's age. Regina was a spaghetti noodle propped up on toothpicks and had dark eyes that always looked sad. Her father had taken off when she was just an infant, so her mother was all she had, until the Baldwins, that is.

The Baldwin home was an enormous Queen Ann that resembled a life-sized doll house. It was three stories of lacy wood siding painted pale green with darker green trim. The home was lavish, complete with a tower in the front with a raised balcony and two porches, all of which were adorned with delicate turned porch posts and ornate spindles. It was such a large house with so few occupants that Dr. Baldwin asked Bessie and her sad-eyed daughter to come live with them. This arrangement pleased all parties. It removed Bessie from a rough area where she and Regina had resided since her husband had vanished in the night, and it also cured the aching solitude Rosela suffered being alone so often in her lonely doll house.

Bessie was a blessing to the Baldwin home. She made it warm and cozy, and for the first time in her life, Rosela started to feel a daughterly bond with someone, and she also grew to love Regina as a sister. Besides keeping up with the household duties, Bessie always made time to play with the girls. She would put music on the phonograph and the three would dance and pretend to sing in their hairbrushes.

Rosela and Regina became all but inseparable. Rosela taught Regina to play the piano and sing, two things Rosela had done since she was six and took great pride in. The school choir was the only activity she participated in, and she loved music more than anything and wanted to share it with her best friend in the world. Eventually the two started playing duets together and putting on little concerts for their parents on the grand piano that took up a large portion of the sitting room. Because both Rosela and Regina suffered from crippling timidity, their intimate recitals were a highlight of their childhood.

For her entire childhood, Regina was Rosela's only friend. The young doctor's daughter found talking to peers as arduous and taxing as lifting an elephant off the ground, and not nearly as entertaining. She had come to the decision that Regina and Bessie were enough for her, and shut herself off from outsiders, more or less.

When she got to middle school and high school, people whispered behind her back about what a recluse she was. After the tenth grade class studied Emily Dickinson and found out about the poet's hermit lifestyle, her classmates started referring to Rosela as "Crazy Emily." She tried to ignore the hateful jeers and focus on her friendship with Regina, but then something awful happened.

"Honey, I need you to sit here next to me," Bessie said to Rosela when she walked into the family room after school. Regina was already in a love seat, her droopy eyes red and swollen.

"What's going on?" Rosela asked, slumping onto the sofa. "What's wrong, Regina?"

"Sweetheart, we got news my mother is ill," Bessie explained. "We're going to have to go to Boston to take care of her."

"What do you mean?"

"I mean we have to go, Rosie. I'm so sorry, but there's no one else to—"

"Can't Regina stay?" she blurted.

"I'm sorry, sweetheart, but she can't."

"Regina?" Rosela said, her eyes trained on her weeping friend.

"I wish I could too," Regina sobbed. "I wish with all my heart I could."

"But you can't just go," Rosela said, looking up at Bessie. "You are my family too. I need you." She broke into tears.

"Oh, Rosie, please don't do this," Bessie pleaded. "I hate this as much as anyone, but my mother needs me now, and it is my duty as her child to be there."

"But what will I do?" Rosela sniffed.

"You'll come visit, and so will we. And Regina will write all the time. I know it will be hard at first, but the pain will ease. And you only have a short time left until you graduate, so who knows what will happen then."

"Yes, who knows," Rosela whispered, and the following week she said good-bye to her best friend, her sister, and the only two people she ever felt comfortable around.

A Miracle

After Regina left, Rosela felt as if a piece of her had died. It was her senior year of school, and she would spend it completely alone. She knew that she was destined to finish high school quietly and without any pomp or circumstance, but then fate flitted down at her feet one brisk March afternoon, quite literally. As she walked home from school, a copy of *The Granician* came sailing across the sidewalk and wrapped itself around one of her frail ankles. Rosela picked up the tattered paper and took it home with her. When she got to her empty doll house, she sat at the breakfast table and skimmed the periodical, and that is when she saw it:

> If you don't have a date for the Senior Prom and are someone who would like to go, please meet in front of the library after school tomorrow night.

It was a small ad peeking out from the upper right-hand corner of the page, posted by a boy named Gerald Bagley. She knew a little about Gerald, but only as much as she could gather sitting behind him in history. He had a nice shaped head and enormous feet, but other than that, he was somewhat of a mystery.

As she read and re-read the ad, she started to consider it. At first she found it absurd, a boy placing an ad in a paper for a date. It was as silly as finding a soul mate in a *Penny Saver*! But the more she thought about it, the more it appealed to her. She knew that no boy was going to ask her to the prom, so this would be her only chance to go. She had wanted just one good memory from high school, and maybe that was it.

What have I got to lose? she thought as she put the paper down and headed out the door for the library.

She was at the library in no time. When she got there, there were three other girls there, one she recognized as a track and basketball star, but the others she didn't know much about. Finally a fifth girl approached them cautiously, and at last the boy with the big feet entered.

"Hello, ladies. My name is Gerald Bagley, but you can call me Giggs. So, would you ladies be interested in going to the Senior Prom?" the boy said, and Rosela could not believe the confidence he had.

"All of us?" a girl with a snaggletooth and close-set eyes asked.

"All of you," he explained. "We'll go not just as a couple, but as five girls and a guy."

Rosela cocked her head and studied this Giggs closely. When she responded to the ad, she didn't quite have a group date in mind. But when she realized that a group date was better than no date at all, she acquiesced. It was official, she was going to prom!

Granite High Cinderella

Because Rosela had never been to a school function, she found that getting ready for the prom was quite a thrilling experience. Her father took an afternoon off work to take her to J.C. Penney so she could pick out a dress.

"You get whatever dress you want, Rosie," Dr. Baldwin said as she poured over the beautiful gowns.

"This is like Cinderella, Daddy," she said as she pulled a gorgeous cream-colored number from the rack.

Rosela tried on seven dresses that day, and finally settled on the perfect one. She was petite, with narrow shoulders and curvier hips, so she picked a mermaid style gown that hugged her pear shape and made her look less like a little girl and more like a young woman. The gown was peach with gold flecks woven throughout so it twinkled when the light hit it just right. When she saw herself in the dress, she felt beautiful for the first time in her life.

With her gown purchased, Rosela waited impatiently for May 1 to arrive. When the calendar showed it was April 29, Rosela felt her shoulder muscles wad into tight little bundles and her stomach seemed to flop in her abdomen. It was her first date ever, and an unconventional one at that, so she was quite nervous.

Regina and Bessie came down for the big day. They could not miss Rosie's first dance ever. The day of prom Rosela paced the house and Regina did her best to soothe her. She also helped her apply her makeup when it came time to do so, as Boston had transformed little, melancholy Regina into a fashionista of sorts. Regina had practiced all night the night before to find Rosela's colors, as she had never worn makeup in her life. The two giggled as Regina smeared hues of blues and greens over Rosie's pale lids.

"I look like a circus clown!" Rosela giggled.

"It's called glamour, Rosie," Regina teased, putting a hand on her jutting hip and sticking her nose in the air. "It's all the rage in the big city."

When it was time to do the real deal, Regina had Rosela's makeup down to an art. She had found the perfect colors—not too much so that Rosela felt like a jester, but enough so that she looked like a striking young woman, ready for her senior prom.

When a shining black limousine came to a stop before the Baldwins' home, Regina and Rosela squealed and threw their arms around one another.

"Don't mess up your hair!" Bessie warned.

"I guess this is it," Rosela said.

"I guess it is," Regina smiled.

"You look like an angel sweetheart," Dr. Baldwin said. "You don't let that boy talk you into any silly stuff."

"Oh, Daddy," Rosela blushed. "We're going in a group. There will be no silliness."

Rosela was the second to last stop, so everyone but Jeanne was in the limousine. Giggs stood and held the door open for her in his black tuxedo, feeling very important.

"That dress is amazing!" Faye exclaimed as Rosela stepped into the car.

"Thank you," Rosela said in almost a whisper.

"No need to be shy, Rosela," Beverly belted. "We're all new friends here."

When they got to the gym Rosela was blown away by the entire event. Being from a well-to-do family, she was accustomed to fresh-cut flowers and fine linens, but the excitement of being around so many people and a live band set her nerves aflame, in a good way. Her skin tingled with nervous excitement.

Although the décor was almost commonplace for the girl who had grown up dining in country clubs and exquisite restaurants with her father and his fellow professionals, Rosela was impressed at how the gym had been transformed. It was so fabulous. The air was filled with music rather than the smell of perspiration and the sound of screeching whistles. There was a live band that was playing big band songs like "Chattanooga Choo Choo" and "Blue Champagne." Giggs led them to a table close to the music, and shortly thereafter snatched up for her first real dance.

It was the first time she had danced with anyone but her father, and what a feeling it was! Rosela wasn't even attracted to Giggs at first, but gliding across the floor with him made her feel even more like Cinderella and he started to look a little more like Prince Charming. She had spent her life in the shadows of her shyness, but finally she had made it to the ball.

After her dance with Giggs was up, one of the second-string basketball players asked Rosela to dance, and she accepted. Everyone but Jeanne spent the rest of the night on the dance floor. Giggs arranged for every pal he had to keep his dates occupied so they would all have the time of their lives. The usually introverted Rosela's head spun as she twirled around the wood floor.

Near the end of the evening, the lead singer in the band lost his voice. The principal of the high school came to the table and leaned to ask Rosela a question.

"I know you have always been in choir. Would you mind filling in for the last song?" he asked.

Rosela didn't have time to think of an excuse, so almost automatically she nodded and followed the principal to the stage, where she sang "Frenesi." The three minutes of singing was like a dream and when she finished the gym exploded into applause.

"That was amazing!" Lois said as Rosela sat back down at the table.

"You could really do something with that voice!" Beverly added.

Giggs dropped Rosela off last that night, which gave the two time to chat one on one. He seemed giddy to her, but perhaps it was just her projecting her own gaiety. Whatever it was, she found there was more to Giggs than his ill-fitting clothes and large feet.

"I never knew you had such a wonderful voice," he told her as they sat beneath the stars.

"Oh, stop," she said as she blushed.

"No, really, I am proud to have been your date tonight. You know, you should do something with your natural talent— you need to follow your dreams and do what you like to do."

Rosela could see Giggs was a dreamer and that he was passionate about doing what he loved. It struck her how sincere he was when he said that to her.

"You know, that has never occurred to me. I've never performed in front of an audience other than my father,

Bessie, and Regina, but that was quite a thrill. I guess it is something I am good at."

"You were born to do it," he said.

"Thank you, Giggs," she replied. "That means a lot."

Right then Giggs leaned in and gave Rosela the most wonderful kiss of her life—the first kiss of her life. Giggs had cracked something open in Rosela—something great.

California Dreamin'

Three months after that amazing prom night, Rosela headed off to college and was scared out of her wits about it. The only place she'd ever really traveled to was Boston, and that was to see Regina. She had decided to pursue a degree in music, and California had the best reputation in the music industry, so she enrolled at UCLA. It was a true adventure for her, and she was not sure that she was ready for it at first.

Once she adjusted to the stark differences between Los Angeles and Salt Lake City, Rosela found that she actually loved everything about LA. It had all the elements necessary for her love of music. She took lessons in clarinet, saxophone, drums, and guitar. She found that she loved the guitar as much as she did piano, if not more, and she took that love and started her own band that she named "Damn Algae" that consisted of Rosela and four of her college roommates.

Rosela completely transformed while in college from a shy introvert to a star. Her father and Regina could hardly believe it as they watched her blossom out in the City of Angels.

After four years and graduation, Rosela started auditioning for other bands. She found a place with a band called The Dorsets that consisted of a skinny, light-haired guy named three young men and Rosela. They became the house band at the Starlight Lounge in downtown LA. One night while finishing up at the Starlight, an agent introduced himself to Rosela and asked if she would like to leave the Dorsets to play piano with the McGuire Sisters. It was an opportunity she couldn't pass up, so she packed her things the next day and started her new career with the McGuire Sisters in New York.

The Big Apple

New York in the 1950s vibrated with hope and dream of grandeur for so many talented folks coming in droves to make it big. The buzz of the city and its hopefuls made Rosela feel both exhilarated and exhausted.

Rosela gained three new sisters and a lifetime of experience playing with the McGuire sisters. The group performed their number one hits on every popular TV show and played all over New York City, but eventually they went their separate ways when one of the girls was linked to famous mobster Sam Giancana.

Rosela went on to do backup work for various performers, but she got her big break one night while playing on the Andy Williams show.

"Would you like to sing with me, Rosie?" he asked. "I need a new backup singer for 'Moon River.'"

It was like prom night all over again.

Rosela went on to work alongside Andy and the two were even romantically involved for a short stint. Rosela branched off from Andy when he met Claudine Longet and their professional relationship came to an end, but she didn't regret the experiences.

Rosela moved to the Plaza Hotel in New York City after that to be in the middle of everything. She had invested most of her earnings over the past ten years in the oil industry, so she was able to reside about anywhere she wanted, and the Plaza Hotel was the perfect place. Conrad Hilton had poured six million dollars into refurbishing it, making it a lavish place to live. There she met the Beatles via Ed Sullivan when they stayed there during their first visit to the United States in February of 1964. She had filet mignon with Ringo Starr and John Lennon. It was hard to believe that this was really her life—a shy girl called Crazy Emily as a teen from Salt Lake City!

Mo Tab

"Geeze, Rosela," Beverly clucked. "They could make your life into a movie!"

"I don't know if it's *that* interesting," she replied bashfully.

"That's more impressive than being gay," Jeanne quipped.

"Stop it, Jeanne," Lois chuckled.

"So do you still sing?" Giggs asked.

"My most recent performing event was with the Mormon Tabernacle Choir in 1978. The director of the choir, Richard Condie, heard me sing back in the sixties with Andy Williams and asked if I would go with the choir to Japan."

"Japan!" Faye exclaimed. "Now that is something!"

When the table quieted, she sighed and said, "Just think, if my lucky stars would not have been with me that day that paper wrapped around my feet, who knows what life would have been like for me. Music is magic," she said as she nodded. "Without music, my life would be so different. Giggs, it was your encouragement that made things possible for me and made me who I am today. To Giggs!" she said, holding up her glass, and again the table joined in.

"And to you ladies too," she added.

Faye Briner

"I don't think anyone wants to have to follow Rosela, so I'll go ahead and take the plunge for us," Faye said as the table quieted.

"You guys are making me blush," Rosela said, swatting at the air with her hand. "It was all good luck."

"I highly doubt that," Jeanne said.

"No, luck doesn't take you that far, Rosie," Lois added. "You worked hard and had talent."

"Okay, okay, enough about me," Rosela said. "Let's hear what Faye has to say before we get kicked out of here."

"Stage is yours, Faye," Beverly said.

"Well, while I hardly became a famous musician, or slept with any," Faye winked at Rosela, "I did have quite a bit happen after that night at prom. In fact, in the last forty years I have experienced a number of events that were triggered by what happened on the night we went to prom."

"You ladies do like to drag things out," Giggs joked. "Let's hear it, Faye!"

Faye was born and raised in a farming family. She was the middle child, with brothers on either side of her and three sisters on either side—two of the sisters were twins. As a little girl, she was a tomboy, but once she hit middle school she shed her denim overalls and slid into dresses with floral patterns and tiny bows sewn to them. Her sisters had always been delicate and dainty, but it took Faye longer to make the jump, and when she did her brothers, Hank and Heath, made fun of her new attire relentlessly.

"What in the world are you wearing, Faye?" they'd mock. "People are gonna mistake you for a girl if you aren't careful!"

"Real funny, you two," she'd snap. "It's a real wonder you don't have girlfriends."

"I don't want a smelly girlfriend," her younger brother, Heath, said as he pinched his nose with his two fingers and stuck out his tongue.

"You will someday," Faye barked. "And when you do, there won't be a girl that'll have you."

"I don't see boys knocking down your door," Hank scoffed.

"So what?" she protested, crossing her arms. "Dad says boys are intimidated by the pretty ones."

"It's that front tooth they're intimidated by," Hank blurted. "No one can get past it!"

"You're just cruel, Hank! You are wicked and mean!" Faye shouted and then turned and ran from the room to escape any further embarrassment.

Faye had been insecure about her pesky tooth since she was nine as it started to slowly protrude, leaving the rest of her teeth behind. She hated to smile in pictures, or any time really, because of the misaligned front tooth, and so if you didn't know Faye you assumed she was grumpy and temperamental, or at least a little sour. Besides her tooth, there was nothing extraordinarily strange about Faye. Her eyes were a little close, but not in a way that drew attention. She was just a plain girl—a plain girl with a snaggletooth.

As Faye became more interested in boys, she also became more sensitive about her looks, particularly her smile. Although there were plenty of other boys and girls with crooked grins, she fixated on hers. She also fixated on the fact that she was the only girl in the family with the dreaded snaggletooth, and also the only girl who didn't have boys drooling over her. Her older sisters, the twins, started going out on dates even before their freshman year in high school. The same was going on now that her younger sister was coming of age. Her little sister, Beth, was as cute as a bug in a rug and the boys were lining up for dates with her.

When no boy ever asked Faye out, she assumed it must have been that cursed tooth. That one little piece of enamel that refused to stand in place with its glossy white cohorts became symbolic for poor Faye. It represented everything she was insecure about: their family's tattered farm house, her worn shoes, the way she had a hard time in math class. She just knew that her jutting front tooth was a tell-all that kept the boys repelled.

Faye really did seem to repel any male suitors. Not a single boy ever asked her to a dance or the movies. She wasn't offensive to the nose, and she could be quite amusing when in the right mood, so the fact that not even the pimple-faced boy who belched all through class seemed to take notice of her started to chip away at Faye's delicate ego. Years of bantering from Hank and Heath had planted a seed, and her invisibility to the opposite sex watered the seed until it blossomed into a nasty plant of self-loathing.

Faye spent her high school years alternating between trying hard to get boys' attention and wallowing in defeat. She found it more and more troubling the way no one approached her. She had never even exchanged a quick accidental glance with a boy in the halls.

"I must be hideous!" Faye blurted as she collapsed on her mother's bed.

"Faye, that is not true," he mother countered.

"It has to be. I am seventeen, Mom. *Seventeen!* And I have never even been asked to the movies, let alone had a boyfriend. I'm probably the only one in my class, Mom!"

"Boys are nothing but trouble, dear."

"I wouldn't know. They don't know that I exist to get me into any trouble."

"It's a blessing, not a curse, Faye."

"Is it?" she demanded. "Is spending my life alone and becoming an old, lonely spinster a blessing?"

"You're being dramatic, dear," her mother sighed. "This is high school. There will be life afterward."

"Most girls know how they will marry by now, or at least they think they do. Not Faye, though. No, sir. It's this tooth," she said, flicking her protruding tooth.

"Honey, I assure you, a tooth is not ruining you."

"So what is?" she demanded.

"Come here, Faye," her mother said, taking her daughter to her hand-me-down vanity. "Look."

"So?"

"Faye, you are a pretty girl. You have beautiful, long, strawberry blond hair. And your eyes, they are so green they shine like emeralds. Your nose isn't mangled or bulbous, and your ears are not flying off your head. And even if they were, you would still be beautiful because that is who you are. You have a beautiful soul. There is nothing wrong with how you look, or who you are. Sometimes it just takes us longer, is all."

"Longer to what?"

"To bloom."

Faye rolled her eyes and sighed, and left her mom's room. Blooming was not her problem. She had already bloomed, she was sure of it. It was just she was a dandelion and not a rose like her sisters. All she wanted was to be a rose, if only for a day.

Unrequited Wishing

The idea of going to a senior prom was special for Faye. She had yet to have been on any sort of date, and so her ego amounted to nothing. Although she would break down to her mother from time to time, she tried not to let anyone else know how she felt. It hurt her feelings that nobody felt she was special enough to ask out. It convinced her that there was indeed some fatal flaw that she possessed.

"Ha! Look at this," Kathy said as she perused that school newspaper at the lunch table. "That boy Gerald Bagley put an ad out for a date."

"What?" Faye asked, nearly choking on her apple.

"It says right here, 'If you don't have a date for the Senior Prom and are someone who would like to go, please meet in front of the library after school tomorrow night.' How peculiar is that?"

"Is it serious?" Faye asked, getting up and looking over Kathy's shoulder.

"I think so. Wait, are you considering this?"

"No," Faye snapped. "I mean, I don't know. Why not?"

"You don't even know him!"

"So?" she said, crossing her arms. "All the boys I do know are already going, so why not?"

"What if he's a creep?"

"Can't be worse than my brothers." She smiled a closed-mouth grin.

"So you're gonna do it?"

"Yeah," Faye said. "I think I am. It's this or no prom at all for me...I'm doing it!"

The Senior Prom was going to be it for Faye. It was her first and only shot at romance before she graduated from high school.

"When does it say to meet?" Faye asked.

"Today," Kathy told her. "I guess after school."

"I'll be there!"

Faye watched the clock closely the rest of the day. When the final bell rang, she made a dash for the library. If this was first come, first served, then she was going to be the first there. When she arrived no one was there, so she took a seat at a table near the entry and waited. Not long after a husky girl named Lois arrived who Faye had in some classes in the past, and then an abnormally tall girl who was a track and basketball star. Two more girls came as well, but still no Gerald. Faye started to think that this whole thing was a hoax, but then suddenly a boy came strolling in and said, "Hello, ladies. My name is Gerald Bagley, but you can call me Giggs. So, would you ladies be interested in going to the Senior Prom?" as he swayed coolly in his polished Oxfords.

"All of us?" she asked, hoping he'd send the others home.

"All of you," he said. "We'll go not just as a couple, but as five girls and a guy."

Faye could hardly believe it. She thought she'd finally be going to prom with a boy, a decent looking boy even, and he was going to take four other girls along!

Faye just blinked and nodded through the rest of the meeting. She agreed to go along with the odd date, but inside her guts felt like they had twisted around themselves. She left the meeting so depressed that when she got home she went straight to her room and cried.

"What is it, hon?" her mom asked as she sat beside her weeping daughter.

"I've spent night after night wishing I could go on a regular prom date," Faye bawled. "Well, we all know where wishing gets you…nowhere!"

"What is going on, Faye?"

"I answered an ad in the paper to go to prom with this boy, but four other girls came and he's taking all of us."

Faye's mother sat for a second and thought, and then said, "Well, I think we should just make the best of it in that case."

"I just wanted it to be special," she sniffed.

"And it can be, if you make it special," her mother said as she ran her fingers through Faye's strawberry blond hair.

Faye decided her mother was right. She straightened up, dried her tears, and set out to make the most of her unusual prom night. She got a beautiful dress from a consignment shop that was powder blue with sheer sleeves that went just off the shoulders and a satin waistband. On May 1, she woke up before everyone else and had a good breakfast. Afterward she went to the beauty parlor to get her hair done, and then she went home where her twin sisters helped her with her makeup.

"You look stunning, Faye," her mother said when she walked in to see Faye in her gown with her hair and makeup done.

"Do you think so?"

"You are going to blow those boys away," she smiled as her eyes glazed with tears.

The First Drink

Just before seven the doorbell buzzed throughout the Briner house. Faye rushed to the door, where her father already stood with a hand on the doorknob. She took a deep breath as she waited for him to open it. There on her front porch was her prom date, dressed up to the tee, with a gorgeous smile.

"Good evening, Mr. Briner," he said as he waited for Faye to join him.

"Hi there, Gerald. You look spiffed up."

"Thank you, sir. I hope you don't mind me saying so, Faye, you look beautiful," he said as he turned to Faye.

"Thank you," she replied as her face burned hot with embarrassment and her heart fluttered.

"This is for you," Giggs said as he handed Faye her corsage that matched her dress exactly.

"It's beautiful!" she swooned.

"For a beautiful lady." He smiled and said, "Shall we?"

"He brought a limousine, Dad!" Faye squealed as she stepped outside and saw the long, sleek car on the gravel drive.

"That's pretty sharp." Mr. Briner nodded. "You have a ball, Faye," he said.

"I know I will!"

With that Gerald escorted Faye out to the car. Inside, the car both Lois and Beverly greeted Faye as she crawled in next to them. They both had on matching corsages as well, and the same enormous grin as Faye.

"Is this fancy or what?" Beverly asked as she rubbed the seat.

"It is amazing," Faye agreed.

The car went by to pick up the last two girls. The final two members of their group date did not seem as excited as the first three. Rosela was next to be picked up, a timid girl who Faye thought looked to be on the verge of throwing up or taking off on foot at any moment. Jeanne, the final girl to join them, just looked terribly uninterested in being there. Faye had heard that she was only going to make a boy jealous, or something like that, so she wasn't surprised that she didn't seem too excited, although she did seem impressed with the mode of transportation.

"I feel like a movie star," Jeanne said as she slid in beside Beverly.

"I know," Beverly replied. "I've never been in a limousine."

Gerald made a comment about Jeanne looking like a movie star as well, which turned Faye off somewhat, but she tried to keep her focus on the excitement of the night.

When they arrived at the dance, Faye was carried through on a cloud of adrenaline and hopeful anticipation. They walked across the beautifully decorated gym as the music the live band played boomed in their ears. They found a table near the band and had a seat. Faye watched as Gerald swept Rosela up and took her to the dance floor. Her heart sank a little as she watched them dance, but Gerald returned and knelt down inches away from her, asking, "May I have this dance?"

"You bet you can," she answered, and she had her first slow dance ever.

Faye was asked by two more boys to dance that night. She could hardly believe it! She had never had a boy notice her, but three boys had spun her around on the dance floor that night. She was in heaven. Her third dance partner was a boy named Jack Dawson, who was known to be a bit of a rebel. When they finished their dance, Jack whispered, "You wanna go out back?" and slid a shining flask out of his inside coat pocket to show her.

"I guess so," Faye said with a little hesitation. She had never even tasted alcohol, but could not find it in her to turn down any kind of attention from a boy.

Faye followed Jack outside, where the two of them took gulps of cheap gin from his flask. It was Faye's first drink ever, and her first swig hit the bottom of her belly and burned hot in her guts. The heat travelled down to her toes and up to the crown of her head and warmed her in such a way that she felt as if she'd been wrapped in a cozy down blanket.

Within a couple of minutes Faye started to feel the effervescence of the liquor bubbling in both her guts and her brain. She felt loose and confident, and all but forgot about her cursed tooth and the number of boys who never knew she existed before that night. Suddenly she felt confident and beautiful and like the life of the party. Faye felt like she had just met her best friend.

The rest of the night Faye felt unstoppable. She chatted away with the other girls at the table. When Rosela was asked to sing the last song, Faye hooped and hollered as she took the stage without any thought to what someone might think of her. The gin worked its magic, giving her a new personality. She wasn't insecure anymore about anything and felt that she was as pretty and important as the prom queen. *I could get used to this,* she thought as she hiccuped into her hand.

When the night was over, the six loaded back into the limousine. Because no one knew Faye that well, her sudden change of demeanor went somewhat unnoticed. She was more talkative than usual and smiled full smiles the entire way to her house. When Gerald dropped her off, she said goodnight, not worrying about spending extra time with Giggs anymore. She had found something better than Giggs—she had found gin!

Lost in the Bottle

Faye continued drinking after prom. She spent the summer working at a restaurant in town, and she fell in with a few older girls who had their own place and liked to hit the town, and the bottle. As the summer passed, she drank more and more, but managed to keep her drinking hidden from her family.

She began dating a guy named Jim who was a cook at the restaurant. He guzzled Coors Original like it was water and he was dying of thirst. Jim had been an all-star football player years before when he was in high school, but for lack of grades and ambition, he never pursued college or a football career. Instead he stayed around the same neighborhood he grew up in and made patty melts and BLTs at the diner and partied every night. Jim was good at interviews, however, so Mr. and Mrs. Briner thought that he was an answer to their prayers, until Jim made such a monumental mistake that their blinders were ripped right off.

One night after their shift ended at the diner, Jim and Faye took off for a party being thrown out near a pond on some farm land outside of city limits. As usual, Jim popped open his first beer the moment they got into his old Ford truck.

"Want one?" he asked Faye as he guzzled the first beer down and reached for another.

"Think we should wait till we get there?"

"Why?"

"I don't know. Just because, I guess."

"Nah. We'll get a head start," he said with a grin.

By the time they made it to the party, Jim was nearly four beers into his twelve pack, and he polished off the other eight before they left, plus a few swigs of whiskey. Faye had cracked open her bottle of gin and so by the time they had to leave, neither of them could recite the alphabet or walk a straight line.

"You sure you're okay to drive?" a friend asked as the two made for the truck, leaning on one another as they went.

"I'm a professional," Jim slurred.

As it turned out, Jim was hardly a professional. He pulled out onto the gravel road and slammed the gas pedal to the floor of the old Ford, spitting dirt and rocks all over the place.

"Geeze, Jim," Faye mumbled as she pressed a bottle of Gordon's gin to her lips and tipped it back.

Jim kept up this way, foot weighing heavy on the accelerator as he barreled down the road. As the speedometer crept upward, Faye's gin haze started to fade.

"Stop sign, Jim!" she called out suddenly, and that was the last thing she said before the front end of a Pontiac buried itself into the driver's side of the truck.

When Faye woke up, she was not wearing her regular clothes. Instead, she was in a dingy white gown. As she blinked her eyes, she realized that she was in a foreign place. The smell of antiseptic and urine told her it was a hospital.

"Faye?" she heard her mother's voice. "Hon, can you hear me?"

Faye groaned and nodded. Her body felt like it had been put into a vice grip and left there for days.

"Hon, you were in an accident, with Jim."

Suddenly Faye remembered the Pontiac and asked, "Is he doing okay?"

"Faye, honey, Jim is gone. I'm so sorry."

"What?"

"He didn't make it, Faye, and neither did the man driving the Pontiac. There are some police here that need to talk to you when you are up to it. It looked like Jim was very intoxicated, Faye. They need to know what happened."

Faye had two options at that point. She could see how close she had come to losing her life and view the loss of her boyfriend and near loss of her own life as a sign from God to get her act together, or she could turn to the bottle to cope with her grief. Faye chose the latter. And she did not just turn to the bottle, she was lost in it.

A String of Bad Luck

Faye went to college the following fall, but she only made it through one year before she dropped out. She left school and she moved in with a man named Rick she met working at a restaurant near the University of Utah, who was as big a drunk as she was. Faye was officially in the wilderness.

Most nights Rick and Faye ended up in heated arguments fueled by cheap liquor. It wasn't uncommon to see Rick with scratch marks across his cheek or his neck after rough nights.

"It was the cat," they'd tell coworkers and family, but strangely they never had mentioned having a cat.

Faye would also turn up with mystery marks—a black eye here and there or a bruise circling her bicep. There was always an excuse, however. They were blacked out more often than not when these things happened, however, so their entire lives became a blur.

After three years of heavy drinking and dysfunctional dating, the two decided to get married. She was, of course, half lit when she made the announcement to her family, who alternated between grieving for and being disgusted by Faye.

The two kept there alcohol-steeped marriage going for about two years before it got to be too much for either of them or gin to handle anymore. After countless fights, a couple of affairs, and a serious come-to-Jesus meeting called by Faye's family, she finally threw in the towel on their marriage.

Faye was still in her early twenties when she and Rick went their separate ways, so she didn't feel too overwhelmed about starting over. She moved into a studio apartment in the Avenues and enrolled in Real Estate school, which she stuck with and finished. She was still drinking heavily, but she was a functioning alcoholic. After school Faye became a real estate broker and found that she was quite gifted when it came to buying and selling property. She worked hard and made a name for herself in the world of real estate, and she eventually met another broker named John. It just so happened that Faye and John had more than just their careers in common. He also loved gin as much as she did.

John was a bit older and had a little girl from a previous marriage, but he didn't see her very often. His ex-wife was very aware of his fondness for drinking, and so only let him see their daughter during holidays and only if his mother or sister was there to drive his daughter because the very last time John dropped his daughter off after a weekend visit two years before, he could hardly walk he was so drunk. His ex was kind enough not to have him thrown in jail, and he was smart enough not to fight her on the custody issue. Being a seasoned alcoholic herself, Faye felt she hardly had room to judge.

Faye and John's relationship was toxic because of their drinking. As time passed, hard liquor seemed to stir bitterness inside both of them and gin sharpened their tongue as it dulled their senses. They went on like that for years, digging deep into any old wound they could sniff out whenever their words slurred and their eyes started to droop. Two times they separated, but as miserable as they were together, they seemed lost without one another. And so they battled on, and the acridity only grew with time until Faye did something that would finally put the last nail in the coffin of their marriage. She went home with another man after a night at the bar. Faye was divorced twice before she was thirty.

The Turn Around

"Well, Faye, I am so sorry to hear all that," Beverly said, suddenly feeling bad about the mimosa she ordered sitting on the table not three feet from Faye.

"Oh, don't be. I got sober in rehab and ended up quitting real estate and getting a beautiful, small place up in the mountains. I just started working at a tack and feed store up there and eventually became the manager. I also got really involved in AA and met my current husband, Clyde."

"In AA?" Jeanne asked.

"Yes, he was my sponsor, but then we realized that there was something between us so I dropped him as a sponsor and picked him up as a beau." She chuckled.

"And everything is going okay now then?" Lois asked.

"Better than ever," Faye smiled. "It's nice being married to someone who gets where I came from. He'd been sober for over a decade when we met, so he was a lot stronger than I was. Plus he knew what to expect with me. It was nice to have someone that could almost predict what I'd do next and help save me from myself."

"He sounds like a catch," Jeanne said.

"Oh, he is. Most of all, though, he makes me feel beautiful and confident without booze. There's just something about him. I've never seen it in another man. He just makes me feel like I'm the only woman in his world."

"That's a pretty amazing thing to find," Beverly said.

"It is. You know, when I think back to prom that night, I could have felt something a lot purer, more like what I feel with Clyde. But I drank that night and got that liquid confidence—that false sense of contentment that fades as fast as the fizz in your head wears off. That night was the first time I ever felt good about myself, and it started with Giggs getting me that dumb corsage and renting that limo to take us in. But then I took a drink, and all that was pushed into the background. It was eclipsed by my buzz. Well, I finally got back to the kind of clearheaded happiness I felt when I first got into that limo, and I want to thank you, Giggs, for being the first to show me what that felt like."

"I wish I could've kept you from that first drink," Giggs apologized.

"Oh hell, Giggs, I was going to take that first drink one way or another. It just happened to be there. Thing is, because of you, when I found happiness sober, I had something to compare it to. I had the first part of that night."

"To Giggs!" Faye said, holding up her water glass.

"To Giggs!" everyone joined in.

Beverly Butterworth

The Wrong Brand of Genes

"All right, all right," Beverly said as she dabbed her eyes with her linen napkin. "We are halfway there now, so I guess that I will go ahead and take the stage, if that is okay with Lois and Giggs, of course," she said, smiling at the two.

"Be my guest," Giggs replied. "I'm really just here to listen. I'm getting a real kick out of all your stories."

"Well, here goes nothing," Beverly said as she drew a deep breath in. "Let's see then. I suppose I will follow suit with you, ladies, and give you all a little background first since no one really knew me before that night at prom. I think it's understood that none of us were exactly in the running for prom queen, but I've never really shared with any of you what brought me to answer that ad Giggs put out."

"Well now is our chance," Jeanne chimed in. "So, Miss Beverly, tell us, what brought you to the library that day?"

Beverly Butterworth, who was known only as "Bev" by her family, spent her childhood wishing that she had never heard of Mrs. Butterworth's Maple Syrup. Although she was as spindly and pale as they came as a kid, no one in her class knew her by anything other than "Aunt Jemima." It got so bad, in fact, that when the teacher would tell one of her classmates to go sit next to Beverly, the student would stand glancing around the room with a confused look on her face.

"Who?"

"Beverly," the teacher would repeat. "Beverly Butterworth. She's been in your class since kindergarten."

"Oh! You mean Aunt Jemima," the girl would say as she glanced over at Bev with a look of accomplishment for having cracked the case.

"That isn't my name," Bev would grumble.

The ill-placed moniker eventually faded, but only to be replaced by something much worse than the name of a maple syrup maid. As Bev got into high school, some of the nastier girls and boys, who by today's standards would no doubt be labeled as bullies, started to call her Butter Butt. The nickname was as misleading as her grade school one, as Bev had grown taller but never any wider. She was awkwardly thin and all elbows, and her backside was as flat as Oklahoma, so the name wasn't just rude, it was also entirely inaccurate. It was just a rather easy and mean nickname to call someone who had the last name of Butterworth.

"They could at least give their teasing a little thought," Bev would complain to her best friend, Tammy.

"Those girls have rocks between their ears," Tammy would say to comfort her friend. "They are hardly worth the energy or frustration."

"I suppose that's easy enough to say when the school doesn't call *you* Butter Butt."

God forbid I ever do gain some weight with a name like Butterworth, she always thought.

Bev had been born and raised in Salt Lake City. Her parents were originally from the Midwest, but headed west looking for work during World War II and settled in Salt Lake City, where her dad worked manufacturing, melding together rails for the Union Pacific Railroad. While many of its residents had settled in Salt Lake City due to the fact that Brigham Young had declared "This is the Place!" to his entourage of Mormons, Bev's dad chose the city for work rather than religion. It was a place where he could get a job to support his family.

Because Salt Lake City consisted primarily of Mormons, families like the Butterworths, who laid down roots there for other reasons and did not practice the faith, were like fish out of water, always struggling for air a bit because of their surroundings. Not being Mormon, Bev always felt that she was an outcast, especially in the last years of her high school career in the late thirties. There were other non-Mormons who went to Granite High School, but the Mormon kids were the smartest, most popular, and also seemed to be the best-looking. Bev started to think Mormons must have excommunicated all the unattractive members, but she soon learned that it was best to keep that theory to herself, as it was not a very politically correct thing to think or say. Either way, no one could dispute that Mormons seemed to have superior genes somehow. If you needed proof, all you had to do was take a look in the Granite High yearbook. The student council, cheerleaders, 4-H leaders, and sports stars were all Mormon.

Bev was finding out how much a religious identity really could make or break a kid, especially in a place steeped so heavily in a particular faith with very particular values. Being Lutheran made her entire school career challenging. Bev had certainly lost the lottery, but it wasn't just the church she belonged to that plagued her. She was not Mormon, a brain, rich, or strikingly pretty. As far as high school went, Beverly Butterworth was nothing, which made her high school experience less than memorable.

Bev always saw herself as "nothing" because she was very vanilla, the type of person who never got noticed and was easily lost in the crowd. She was a sinewy five feet, five inches, and had mousy brown hair and rust-colored eyes with a nose she always considered too big for her narrow face. She also wore glasses. On top of her average-at-best features, Bev rarely wore any makeup to accentuate anything, except for the occasional lipstick or rouge she would "borrow" from her mother's bureau when she wasn't around.

Bev's family was also very frugal, which others took to mean they were poor. Her parents didn't believe in buying anything that wasn't a basic necessity, so she never had anything that was in style. As far as clothes, the Butterworths got what was needed to cover their bodies and keep warm. The new style of dresses showed off curves and the feminine body, gathering in to define the waistline with tops that had butterfly or puffed sleeves. All the girls in her class wore calf-length dresses with flowing sleeves and a defined empire waistline, while Bev was stuck wearing long, dull-colored dresses to cover her knock-knees. Her clothes hung like burlap on wire hangers over her body. She felt like a rag doll most of the time whose stuffing had been pulled out. Mary Jane shoes also became all the rage, and when all the other girls started wearing them, she was left with only her black and white saddle oxfords.

"When those are worn through, we'll talk about a new pair," her father told her when she begged for her own pair of Mary Jane's.

"But these shoes make me even more of a bore than I already am," she protested.

"Clothes don't make you a bore, Beverly Butterworth. Lack of character does," her father scolded.

"You just don't understand high school now, Daddy," she pouted. "If I *look* boring, then I *am* boring. People don't give you a chance if you don't look the part."

"I don't know that I'd want to associate with such petty people," her father replied with an eyebrow raised. "There are important things in life, Bev. Mary Jane's are not one of them."

"But they *are* in high school, Daddy," she whined. "I am already an outcast as it is. Please!"

"This won't mean a thing to you some day, Bev," her mother interjected. "High school is a very small piece of a very big puzzle."

Bev tried to take comfort in her mother's reassurance, but found it hard to believe that her plainness wouldn't follow her around like an unwanted shadow. As much as she wanted to believe that high school was nothing, she had a terrible feeling that it was just the first act, and that all acts that followed hinged on what role you landed before the play even started. That was an uncomforting thought because so far she was hardly even a spectator, let alone a leading lady.

The Last Chance

Although Bev was hardly excited about going to school, she moved through the motions as she counted down the days to graduation, at which time she could move on into adulthood and hopefully leave high school, and maybe even Utah, behind her. She bumbled along, quietly ducking the girls and boys who called her Butter Butt as they passed, and soon became all but invisible. No one other than Tammy ever noticed or cared about her because she had made herself so

Dr. Melvin J. Bagley

very unnoticeable. Her invisibility became a double-edged sword. While she evaded teasing, she also fell off the radar so completely that she was never asked out by a boy, and rarely invited to any gathering.

As Bev approached the bottom of the ninth in the big game of high school, her anonymousness became almost too much to bear. There was one major event left, the high school prom, and while she was never the type to particularly care for dances, she wanted nothing more than to get to go to this one last monumental occasion. The problem was that a girl had to be invited by a Granite High senior to go to the prom, and Bev was almost certain that the only boy who even knew her real name was a kid named Gordon in her chemistry class who always cheated off her. Besides that, the prom was not a place for girls like her—it was for the popular, pretty girls, girls whose families had money to buy them nice gowns. As far as she could tell, going to prom was as much a possibility for her as walking on the moon, until one chilly Monday rolled around.

As Bev sat in the school library, as she was prone to do because she had nowhere better to go, she noticed a tiny ad in the corner of one of the pages of the school newspaper.

> If you don't have a date for the Senior Prom and are someone who would like to go, please meet in front of the library after school tomorrow night.

As she read the short ad again and again, she felt her pulse quicken. *Could this be true?* she wondered. She had resigned to the fact she would not be attending prom. But as she sat there and studied the little corner of that newspaper page, optimism settled in her brain. The letter was vague, but Bev got the impression that there must have been a pool of boys who wanted to go to the prom who were meeting girls who didn't already have dates to pair off for the big dance. Although she was hesitant at first, she decided that it was her last chance, so she was going to show up at the library to see if maybe she'd find someone who might make the very last of high school something special for her. She hoped for a Prince Charming, but was willing to settle for a polite boy her age with a decent smile.

When Beverly arrived at the library that evening, she was thrown for a loop. She had expected a group of boys standing in a line, waiting for the girls to arrive and pluck them one by one like dandelions from a flower bed. Instead she came up on four other girls waiting with confused looks on their faces. There was a very tall girl, an obvious athlete; a pudgy girl; an average looking girl whose hand seemed glued to her lips; and a very petite girl who was quite cute but looked to be scared of her own shadow. Bev walked over to the eccentric little group. As they all looked around bewildered, a single boy finally appeared.

"Hello, ladies. My name is Gerald Bagley, but you can call me Giggs. So, would you ladies be interested in going to the Senior Prom?" he asked as he swayed in place and studied the girls.

"All of us?" the girl with the hand hovering in front of her lips asked. Although she seemed to stay hidden behind that one hand, she was the most assertive of the introverted bunch.

"All of you," he nodded. "We'll go not just as a couple, but as five girls and a guy."

When Bev heard Gerald's response she felt her face turn hot and her vessels tighten under her skin. She surmised that this Bagley fellow must have pitied the girls without dates, and the last thing she wanted was to be pitied by some slimy boy! She felt indignant not just for her, but for the other girls as well. She was neither jealous nor envious of them. She felt nothing but camaraderie with the girls there that day that were also offered a pity date. She could hardly stand it!

Bev looked at the four others and tried to read their reactions. She figured that they, like her, were probably wondering what all the others would do. She sat quietly and mulled it over. It was not at all what she had expected and she was hardly pleased with the arrangement.

"You all don't have a date, and neither do I," Gerald said, breaking the silence. "If I take you all, we can all at least get into the prom and have a chance at a good time. I'll take all five of you and make sure you're night is something special— at least more special than sitting at home on our rumps. Some of the most popular boys will be there, you know? Who's to say they won't come over and dance with you?"

"Sounds a little nutso, Giggs," the same girl who had spoken up earlier said.

"Yeah, it does," Beverly said with some venom in her words.

"What have we got to lose?" Giggs asked.

One by one, all the other girls agreed that they would go to the prom with Gerald. As Beverly watched each girl nod her head and join in, she felt red hot rage churning in her guts. Any bit of dignity she had was being burned up in the moment that one big-footed boy with glasses and a large nose just like hers stood rocking on his skis with the audacity to ask five girls out. She began to tell Gerard thanks, but no thanks for the invitation to the prom. *Who does he think he is?* she fumed. *Some kind of God's gift to women?*

The thing about Gerald was that he really didn't *act* like he thought he was something special. He just acted excited at the prospect of helping all of the girls who didn't have dates get to their prom. He had self-confidence, Bev could see that, but he didn't seem smug or self-important.

Bev was torn. She was not sold on the idea of a group of outcast girls going on a big date with one not-so-popular guy, but deep down she did want to go to the prom. So finally she caved and agreed to go.

I Feel Pretty

Once Bev made the decision to go, her next big issue was deciding what to wear, and more importantly, where in the world she'd get it. The Butterworths were as tight as a muscle cramp on a swimmer when it came to money, so she knew that there was no way that they were going to spend money on an expensive dress that she would only wear one time.

"What'll I do for a dress?" Bev asked her mother one evening as she flipped through a *Time* magazine.

"What about Lucy?" her mother said.

"What about her?"

"Well, she went to prom a couple of years ago. Maybe you could borrow her dress."

"How in the world would I even ask that, Mom?" Bev sighed. "Lucy and I aren't even close."

Lucy was the daughter of Mrs. Butterworth's good friend, Opal, and although she was nice enough, she and Bev had never been that great of friends. She had no issue wearing a hand-me-down dress, but she did find it mortifying just thinking of asking Lucy to borrow it.

"I'll just ask Opal, hon. I know she'll be fine with it."

True to her word, Bev's mother asked about the dress and both Opal and Lucy were more than happy not just to let Bev borrow the dress, but to give it to her. Lucy was shorter and heavier than Beverly, so the gown had to be altered, but when it was taken in and some length was added, it truly was lovely: a light blue number with white lace trim. Even with her glasses, flat hair, and awkward stance, Bev actually felt pretty when she was wearing the dress.

"How does it fit, Bev?" her mom asked over the fitting room door.

"I feel...pretty," she answered.

After that, Bev eagerly awaited for the night of the dance to arrive, not as much to be with Gerald, but for the experience of going to a prom wearing such a pretty gown.

The big night arrived and Gerald picked his dates up one by one in the polished limousine. Bev was the second person to be picked up, right after a big-boned girl named Lois. When the limousine pulled in front of the Butterworth house, Bev's heart nearly exploded from excitement.

"That is very nice, but I really don't see why that boy spent so much on a car," Mr. Butterworth said as he shook his head.

"Hank," Mrs. Butterworth scolded. "This is a special night. It's stunning, sweetie," she said, turning to her glowing daughter. "Now go have a good time!"

Giggs introduced himself to the Butterworths, presented Beverly with a light blue corsage, and then escorted Beverly to the waiting car. Just before Bev climbed in next to Lois, Giggs was sure to tell her, "You look like a million bucks tonight, Beverly Butterworth."

"Geeze, Gerald," Bev replied, blushing hard. "Thank you. I really like your tuxedo too."

"It's fancy, isn't it?" Lois interjected as Bev sat beside her.

"It sure is," she said, glancing around the back of the limousine. "I never imagined I'd be taking a limousine to prom."

"That makes two of us." Lois chuckled.

The night started out like a dream for Beverly, but as soon as they arrived at the dance the vision she had of herself as some beautiful swan quickly vanished when she saw all the other girls in their gorgeous gowns and fancy hairdos. They were the cool, serious beauties who cast disdainful looks around the hallway at people like her. Suddenly Bev felt awkward in the fancy dress and had a compulsion to run away, but quickly realized she had no way to get home and it was too far to walk.

While Bev wrestled with her crippling insecurity, Gerald was beaming as they walked across the decorated gymnasium. He was obviously very proud of taking five girls to the prom.

The group sat down at a table near the band and Gerald immediately asked the quiet Rosela to dance. He eventually asked Bev to dance as well. She thought he was nice enough and appreciated the sentiment, but she really didn't feel any kind of attraction to him and was glad when her dance with him was over. As the night wore on, Bev danced with one other boy, but when Bev could see that the boys coming over obviously felt some sort of moral obligation to dance with the outcast girls because of an arrangement with Giggs, she did not appreciate it too much, so she put her head down when she felt one of the boys coming her way. She noticed that Jeanne did the same and figured that she must have had the same idea.

Bev sat next to Jeanne and Lois, and at first not a single one of them said a thing that was more than a necessary nicety.

"You look very pretty."

"I love your hair."

"That dress is something."

Short, quick, polite sentences were mumbled in an attempt to break the awkward silence. But then Lois said something funny about the whole situation with the five-to-one ratio between girls and the boy.

"We're just living up to the myth that all Utahans are polygamists," she joked.

With that the ice was broken and the entire table cracked up. After that, everyone started talking, really talking. And Bev's world opened as it never had before. Bev soon realized that she was having a much better time just getting to know the girls at the table than she ever would dancing with some boy she didn't know. It was strange, she thought, how they became the highlight of the prom for her.

A New World for Bev Butterworth

The girls began to talk about common interests, their families, the songs they liked best, which teachers they despised the most, future plans for college or work, and, most importantly, which boys everyone thought were the cutest. Bev was much more interested in the conversation that had commenced at the table than dancing or boys. The five girls had never been overly talkative in school. Years of harassment had rendered them a rather close-tongued lot, until then.

Bev had always had a bit of a self-deprecating sense of humor, and she began telling the others how awkward she felt in her dress as her knees literally banged together when she walked. Slowly, each one of the girls began telling about how they felt ugly, fat, unpopular, snaggletooth, boring, or just all-around different. As the girls talked, Bev realized that they all had a few traits that made them feel less attractive, and therefore less popular, along with other tribulations that made their lives a bit more difficult.

Once they got going, it was hard to get a word in edgewise. Everyone had so much to say. Lois told of how she used her excess weight to torture her siblings.

"When they pick on me I grab them and sit on them. That always shuts them up," she said with a wicked grin.

Faye admitted that she had just snuck out with a boy and had her first drink.

"It just made me feel better for once, you know? It's like it soothed my soul." But then, with a sinful smile, she added, "It really is great though, you all should give it a try."

Jeanne didn't say much, except that she just never felt like a girly girl and always felt like she didn't fit in. "I just don't really care for all the dramatics of boys, you know?"

Even the timid Rosela admitted to writing anonymous letters to some of the mean girls in their class, letting them know what a horrible effect their words and actions had on others.

Bev had been a little reluctant to share too much at first, but she found that the more everyone shared, the easier it became. It was strangely comforting to know they all had common feelings of inferiority. It was almost uplifting to know that she was not alone in her sense of negative self-image. As the girls began to detail these feelings, it turned out they all had one thing in common—the desire to be "normal." And the more they talked the more they realized that perhaps they *were* the normal ones!

"We're all kind of the same," Bev smiled. "Not with our backgrounds, or beliefs, or struggles so much, but in the way we feel we are viewed by others."

Bev had kept her feelings tucked away far too long and that night they came out in waves.

"You guys know that song, 'It's Not Easy Being Me'?" Bev asked, and the table nodded collectively. "I always identified with that. You know, I felt no one understood what it was like to be an outcast. But now I don't feel so bad about it."

The evening became a clarifying time for her, and she imagined it did for the others as well. Some of the other girls at the dance started looking at the five girls jabbering away with a bit of envy as they tugged on their uncomfortable dresses and tried to look perfect. Bev noticed those furtive glances and thought they were probably envious deep down of the good conversation and fun they were having. They might have been prettier and the big shot athletes, but most likely they were unhappy about something: their appearance, their date, their back-biting friends. Who knew?

The five girls at the table were having fun, not pretending to have fun, but truly having fun. They laughed heartily, but there were also heart-rending confessions. Each had at one time or another been the brunt of unkind words. The name-calling, the eye-rolling, the sneering, and the flat-out mean statements of others had hurt the girls to the core and a few tears were shed, but they combated the bad memories with laughter and did not dwell on the events.

Bev had always felt she had two personalities: one that was an introvert and very quiet and one that more outgoing, who loved to make people laugh. She went on to show the girls what she referred to as her "monkey face." They all agreed that she could pass for a tenant in the nearby zoo. It really got the table going and soon they were all telling stories and laughing. All of the negative feelings they had toward themselves were being transformed into comedy routines.

The dance lasted four hours, but it seemed must shorter because so much happened in that time. What had started as a night of trepidation ended in a night of enlivening conversation and many, many smiles.

Parting Ways

The meetings of Gigg's Girls forever changed Bev's life. It was there she realized for the first time that she was not alone in her feelings and that these other girls who were not seen as outstanding to others were smart, witty, and had very good hearts. Her self-esteem raised by leaps and bounds that last month of school.

Even with her new friendships formed, when it came time to graduate Bev was thrilled she would never have to step foot in that high school again. She did like some of her classes and teachers, but she was glad to know that Granite High, and that feeling of being awkward and unknown, would soon be in her past. She knew that her newborn friendships with Faye, Lois, Jeanne, and Rosela were going to change. They were all moving on toward whatever the rest of their respective lives would bring. But no matter what, they would always be Gigg's Girls.

After she graduated from Granite High, Bev went to community college. She didn't have much money throughout college and she lived on Campbell's soup, but she didn't know any different and loved those days. She was Granite High-free and blissful about it.

Not long into her first semester, Bev met a boy named Melvin who was handsome and as charming as they came. If she wasn't studying, she was on a date with Melvin. He, like Bev, was also dirt poor, so their dates usually consisted of early morning fishing trips to Strawberry Lake out by Midway.

As Bev got older, her plain looks transformed into something very pleasant. Her nose may have been a little too big still, but she grew to love even that. It was, after all, her only nose! That stopped mattering to Bev, however. As she got older, the memories of popularity and nasty girls evaporated into all the greatness of the present. Bev became happy with her life.

After graduating from community college, she became a secretary in a law office and rose in the ranks to eventually become the office manager, which was and still is a job she loves.

Bev went on to marry one of Melvin's friends, Glade, and they had four children: three girls and a boy. She came to realize that her mother was right years before when she told her that high school was a very small piece of a very large puzzle. She only wished that she could have known how great the puzzle would look.

It's Been Too Long

"Well now we know why I didn't care for boys' drama," Jeanne said and laughed.

"I had almost forgotten that we spilled the beans like that," Faye said. "Too many gin and tonics, I guess," she said with a wink.

"We sure did," Bev replied. "It was the best day of my high school career—one of the best in my life probably."

"Yes, we were 'Gigg's Girls,'" Lois said.

"We were," Bev agreed as her head bobbed on her neck. "Still are, I guess."

"I sometimes forget how bad high school was," Rosela said as she twirled her salad fork on the linen tablecloth.

"Yes, we all got our fair share of abuse," Bev said." You know that is considered bullying now. They didn't call it that then, but it can have devastating consequences."

"I don't know about you all, but the more we talked that night, the more I realized that all that terrible stuff we thought about ourselves—all that stuff others made us feel—was wrong," Faye said.

"It was dead wrong!" Bev exclaimed. "We were as good as anyone back then and still are!"

"And you were almost too fired up to even go with me that night," Gerald added.

"I certainly was," Bev sighed. "I was always on the defense because of how I was treated, I guess. Plus I didn't know you from Adam, and there you were, asking five girls to prom!"

"It worked out though, didn't it?"

"I'd say it did, you old coot. We got to listen to each other, and make something pretty amazing with the quirkiness each one of us brings to the table."

"I feel a little left out of the loop," Gerald joked.

"Well, I always thought of you. It was you, after all, who changed my life when you had the harebrained idea fifty years ago to ask five girls to the prom."

"Harebrained ideas can be a good thing. That wasn't my only one, that is for sure, but it may have been my best one."

"That one particular event forever changed my attitude toward myself, my feelings toward others, my relationships, and essentially my life," Bev said as her eyes went glossy.

"It changed us too, Bev," Jeanne said as she reached her hand toward her friend to comfort her. "It really did."

"When I was younger, I considered myself ugly. I was never ugly."

"I can't believe you ever thought that," Lois said.

"What I can't believe is that I was *this close* to backing out of the most beautiful, funny, painful, and life-changing experiences I have ever had," Bev said. "The tears of anguish shared over our own stories of self-doubt that night have changed to tears of love and happiness. I can't thank you all enough. Or you, Giggs, for bringing us together. To Giggs!" Bev said, raising a toast.

"To Giggs!" the other four exclaimed.

6

Lois Wright

"That leaves just you, Lois," Beverly said once everyone's glasses were back on the tabletop.

"It looks like it does," Lois replied. "It has been so great listening to everyone that I almost forgot that I had not yet told my own story."

"Yes, ma'am," Faye chirped. "I told you all what a drunk I was, so now it is your turn!"

"Well," Lois said as she glanced around the table, "you all can see just from looking at me one of the big changes that happened in my life."

"We absolutely can!" Jeanne exclaimed. "You look just wonderful, Lois."

"You sure do!" Beverly agreed. "You were always beautiful, don't get me wrong, but you look better then ever."

"Thank you so much," Lois said as her cheeks flashed a rosy tint.

"So," Faye said, "tell us everything. I mean, I think we all know some, you being a local celebrity and all, but we want to hear the parts that the TV and the news write-ups didn't tell us back when you got your crown."

"I remember when I heard it," Giggs broke in. "That Lois Wright was crowned Miss Utah. I couldn't believe it. I took Miss Utah to senior prom. Now how many fellas can say that?" Giggs asked with an eyebrow raised.

"Not just Miss Utah," Rosela corrected. "Miss *America*."

"So, do tell the rest," Jeanne insisted.

∽✖✑∾

Her senior year, Lois Wright suffered the most devastating loss that a teen could; the loss of her mother. For years Lois's mother had been battling breast cancer. In February of 1940, nearly four years after the awful diagnosis shook their family, Yolanda Wright lost her battle just months before her daughter was set to graduate from high school. Just before she died, Yolanda called Lois into her bedroom.

"Yes, Mama?" Lois said as she slipped onto the bed beside her frail mother.

"I know this is not easy to hear, but my time is not long now, Sweet Lois," her mother said. "You have been a very good daughter, and you have cared for me like no one but a daughter could. I want you to do something for me when I am gone though."

"Anything you say, Mama," Lois said as tears gathered in her big, brown eyes.

"I want you to finish your studies."

"Yes, Mama. I will."

"I mean this, Lois. Education is one thing that no one can take from you as a woman."

"I promise I will," Lois assured her mother.

"And you make sure that your brothers do too. You will be the head of the family, my sweet. I know it will be hard at times, but you will do right by them, I know."

Six years before when Lois was only twelve years old she had lost her father to a sudden heart attack. Her father was the sole reason her family was in Utah—it was his birthplace. Lois's mother was from the Philippines and had met her father, Jackson Wright, while he was there teaching English. Lois was beautiful and the kindest person Jackson had ever met. The two fell in love, married, and immediately had their first child, a little girl named Lois, Jackson's grandmother's namesake. The couple went on to have two more boys over the next five years.

When Lois was eleven, the family moved back to her father's homeland and started their life there. Just a year after they had set down new roots, Jackson's heart stopped beating as he stood in an elevator headed for his office floor. It was just her, her mother, and her two younger brothers left. Now, however, it was clear that soon it would just be Lois and her brothers. Her heart ached at the thought of having neither parent left at so young an age.

Yolanda took her last breath on a sunny, late February morning as the biting cold blocked any warmth of the sun from getting to the frozen Utah ground. The day her mother passed, Lois sat stunned for the entire day. She stayed that way throughout the wake and funeral, but as they lowered her mother into the rectangle hole in the ground, finally something broke inside of the heartbroken girl. As Lois let go a handful of earth onto her mother's shining casket, she fell to the ground as waves of violent sobs overtook her entire body. Lois cried from depths she never knew were there inside her. She cried until her lungs nearly collapsed and her entire body was trembling. And she didn't stop crying for weeks.

At school, Lois walked the halls like a robot. As all the other girls giggled and talked about who had asked them to prom and what kind of dress they were going to wear, Lois grieved the loss of her mother inwardly. Going to the prom was the last thing on her mind. Even if she hadn't just lost her only living parent, no boy had ever noticed her, so she wouldn't have been going anyway.

Lois had always kept to herself. She had a heavy Filipino accent that she tried to hide and she also struggled with her English at times. Beyond her language barrier, she had also been chunky since she was just a child. Lois struggled with her weight throughout middle school and high school. She had a couple of friends in school, but never once had a boy showed any interest in her, unless of course he was teasing her for her weight or the way she spoke. Lois learned to ignore the juvenile banter of the silly boys. Her mother and father had provided her with a loving home and taught her that people who said and did mean things were not worth worrying about, so she cared little what others had to say.

Even with her amazing mother and father gone, Lois still had a great home. Her Aunt Cel and Uncle Greg, who also lived in Salt Lake City, took her and her brothers in and provided them a wonderful home. The love that her aunt and uncle showed helped Lois tremendously, but still she missed her mother with all her being. She missed her so much that she could care less that her senior prom was fast approaching and she had no date. She could not imagine having fun at that time of her life anyway.

One day as Lois sat in study hall and read through the school newspaper, a strange ad caught her attention. It read, "If you don't have a date for the Senior Prom and are someone who would like to go, please meet in front of the library after school tomorrow night."

How odd! Lois thought as she stared at the tiny ad. She started to dismiss it and go on about her day, but something about it intrigued her. Why would someone put that in the school paper? And who was that someone, anyway? After a little debate as to whether or not it was worth investigating, Lois decided that she would go check it out. She had done nothing but cry for weeks, so perhaps it was time to go on with life.

When she got to the library that evening, there was one other girl there who looked to be waiting as well. Lois smiled at the girl with strawberry blond hair, and the girl smiled back a very faint smile that didn't show her teeth. The two did not talk. Soon three others trickled in. Lois recognized one girl as a track star and one girl she had heard other kids picking on for her name in the halls—they called her Butter Butt, which Lois found odd because the girl was rail thin.

Eventually a boy appeared who Lois recognized as Gerald Bagley. She had him in a couple of classes, but had never exchanged so much as a "hello." He had never been one of the boys to pick on her, however, so she assumed he was at least a decent young man.

"Hello, ladies. My name is Gerald Bagley, but you can call me Giggs," Gerald announced. "So, would you ladies be interested in going to the Senior Prom?"

"All of us?" the girl who had been there first asked.

"All of you," he explained. "We'll go not just as a couple, but as five girls and a guy."

Lois didn't know what to think about the request. She had come with no expectations, really, but she had not expected a group date to be the outcome. She sat quietly and tried to take it all in, and then Gerald went on.

"You all don't have a date, and neither do I. If I take you all, we can all at least get into the prom and have a chance at a good time. I'll take all five of you and make sure you're night is something special—at least more special than sitting at home on our rumps. Some of the most popular boys will be there, you know? Who's to say they won't come over and dance with you?"

"Sounds a little nutso, Giggs," the same girl said, and Lois noticed she had a little bit of a snaggletooth that she thought made her look very unique.

"Yeah, it does," the girl named Butterworth added.

"What have we got to lose?" Gerald asked.

The more Gerald talked, the better the idea became to Lois. Her uncle had warned her boys could get fresh on dates when they were alone with girls, which could ruin her dream of finishing school.

One by one all the girls agreed that they would give the group date a shot. Lois was almost surprised at how willing she was to go. She hadn't even cared about the prom the day before. She went home and told her family. Her Aunt Cel and Uncle Greg were thrilled at the news. They had been worried about her since her mom had passed and were happy to hear she was going to her prom.

The next week Lois found herself stressing about where she would get a dress for the prom, but her Aunt Cel swooped in to the rescue when she told her niece that she would call her seamstress and have Lois a dress made just for her.

Lois was off to see the seamstress the next day and just one month later, she picked up a long, lavender gown with a sheer overlay. When Lois tried it on for the first time, she could hardly believe her reflection. The dress was beautiful, and so was she.

When the big day finally arrived, Lois's beautiful cousin Bernadette helped her get ready. She swept shimmery eye shadow over her cousin's eyelids the color of honey and brushed just enough blush on her cheeks that she looked as if she were slightly blushing. After makeup, Bernadette curled all of Lois's silky black hair and then pinned her shining curls so that she looked just like Bette Davis. With her hair and makeup done to perfection, Lois put on her dress and she felt like Bette Davis too.

When the doorbell rang Lois felt her mouth go dry and her knees start to shake. Her stomach felt like she was on a roller coaster that just kept dropping. *Take a deep breath*, she told herself as her head felt like it was full of helium. Lois closed her eyes, counted to four, and headed to see her first date ever. When she made it to the family room, there stood Gerald, a perfectly purple corsage in hand and a smile on his face. He was wearing a black tuxedo. Lois felt as if she were living someone else's life all of a sudden, all dolled up with a sharp-dressed man waiting to whisk her away.

"Hi, Gerald," she said bashfully.

"Well, hello, Miss Wright," Giggs replied, trying to sound as proper as he could. "You look just like a dream."

"Thank you so much," she said. "You look quite handsome as well."

"I clean up okay," Giggs replied with a grin. "Shall we?"

"Oh, yes, of course," Lois stuttered, and off they went.

"Have her home by midnight, Gerald," Uncle Greg called after them as the two were leaving.

"Yes, sir," Giggs replied over his shoulder with a little salute.

Seeing with New Eyes

Lois lived the closest to Gigg's house, so she was the first girl for him to pick up. When Lois saw the beautiful, black limousine that shone like onyx in the late spring sunshine, she could hardly contain her giddiness. She never in her wildest dreams imagined going to her senior prom in a limousine.

Lois slid into the gigantic backseat and took in all the details that surrounded her—the plush seats and glossy finish on all the hard surfaces in the car. As she settled in, she felt nervous anticipation fizzing up in the depths of her stomach. She was anxious to see what prom was like—what the décor, music, and even the people there looked like. She was also eager to see what the other four girls were wearing that would be accompanying her and what their demeanor would be. Would they be as thrilled as she was? This was a world Lois Wright had never stepped foot in, so every part of it was an adventure.

They picked up Beverly next, the thin girl who they called Butter Butt at school, and then the strawberry blond girl named Faye, who looked to have been in a farming family by her house. After that was Rosela, whose picturesque Victorian doll house mesmerized Lois. Finally, they picked up the track star, Jeanne Whitehead. One by one the girls piled into the car. Each girl looked breathtaking in her own unique way.

Lois knew little to nothing about the girls in the group. When she first agreed to do the group date, she wondered what each girl was like. As they talked on the ride there, it was still difficult to read her co-dates. But after the girls relaxed a bit and worked through the awkwardness of breaking the ice, Lois realized how much she liked the four girls sitting with her. She liked them so much, in fact, that she was more interested in talking to them than in the magnificence of the senior prom.

In the school gymnasium, Lois was surrounded by beautiful floral arrangements made of fresh cut hydrangeas and pale roses. The sound of live music floated through the air, but the conversation taking place at their table near the band eclipsed all of that. Lois was intrigued as she sat listening to everything the others had to say. She found that Beverly was quite eloquent and passionate when she spoke, and that Rosela, though painfully shy at school, was a captivating individual. At first Lois said little as the others discussed things, like being picked on at school and boy problems. Because of her heavy accent, she had learned to say little in conversations, but she found that after a while with the four girls, the insecurity about her sometimes shaky English faded into the amenity of the group.

As Lois got to know more about the girls, and their very different, but equally delightful personalities, she started to wonder how none of them had dates. She knew all the reasons she had no date. First and foremost, there was her size, but there were also other factors Lois knew kept her from ever getting asked out by a boy. She had been taking care of her mother since high school began and had no time for socializing or flirting with boys. She was far too busy caring for her mother, tending to her brothers, or studying to focus on anything else. Faye, Beverly, Jeanne, and Rosela didn't seem to have any of the same problems that Lois could see, so she marveled at the fact that the boys in their class were too dim to see how amazing her new friends were.

Lois didn't just sit and talk all that night, she also danced, first with Giggs, but he was not the only one. Just one song after she had waltzed with Gerald around the dance floor, a boy named Tommy Evans came over to the table. Tommy was one of the popular boys in the senior class and Lois had always found him particularly handsome. Beyond that, he was a gentleman. He, like Giggs, had never bullied her about her weight or the way she talked. That night he went right up to the usually overlooked young woman and asked, "May I have this dance?"

"You may," she replied timidly.

Lois felt uneasy at first as she and Tommy took to the floor. The only other time she had danced with a boy before, besides her brothers and cousins at wedding celebrations, was the dance she just had with Giggs. She was certainly a novice on the dance floor, and there she was, hand in hand with a gorgeous boy. As she slipped her hand into his, it trembled.

"Everything will be okay," Tommy assured her, noticing how shaky she was.

Lois smiled and started to calm down. As her pulse slowed, everything else seemed to even out and her dance went very well. When the song was over, Tommy walked her back to her chair and said, "Thank you very much for the dance," and then pressed his lips to Lois's plump cheek.

Lois thought of the dance and the peck on the cheek for some time. Her skin tingled where Tommy's lips had pressed into it. As she sat down quietly, a strange feeling came over her, a feeling she had never experienced before in all her life. It was almost like she was in another world and something strange had happened. Even though Lois was a hundred pounds heavier than the other girls at the table, for the first time in her life she felt like she belonged. It was like she was seeing the whole world with new eyes.

After Lois regained her composure and was able to concentrate on what was going on around her again, she glanced over at the dance floor. She saw Tommy with his date, who was slim and curved in all the right places, and thought, *Somehow that could be me.* For the first time ever, Lois felt as if she too could be someone—someone beautiful, someone lovely, someone others cared to know, someone who could do anything she set her mind to. With a brand new confidence burning in her chest, Lois spent the rest of the evening chatting, laughing, and nearly crying with her friends.

On the way home Lois was quiet as could be. For some reason, she did not want the other girls to find out how much pleasure she took in that dance with Tommy. She knew that it would sound just ridiculous, but that night she started to dream of someday being with the hunky Tommy Evans.

The Lucky Charm

The night of senior prom changed Lois's life forever. Lois came to the conclusion that it was time to make some lifestyle changes that would help her become the person she wanted to be. She had her own kind of confidence and believed in herself because of the self-worth her family had instilled, but she realized that she was doing herself no favors by staying overweight. It was time to change that!

"I want to lose this weight," she told her aunt the day after her senior prom.

"Well, hon, getting into shape would make you feel much better. But can I ask, what made you decide this all of a sudden?"

"I just realized something at prom," she said. "I want to be a better me. I want to feel good about all the parts of me. I cannot do that if I am a hundred pounds too big."

"You just tell me what you need from me, Lois, and I will do all I can," her aunt told her.

For the next couple of months Lois dove into her new mission. She tried several weight loss programs, but nothing seemed to work. She tried the things the stars supposedly did, and she even tried not eating at all, but all to no avail. Then one day she stumbled across a new kind of program. The way it worked was fairly simple: she would only eat fresh foods, nothing processed, no breads, fats, or sugar. She just ate good foods and ate them in moderation. On top of that, she included daily exercise for at least thirty minutes.

Over the next six months Lois saw drastic differences in her body and her energy. She lost fifty pounds and felt physically and mentally better than she ever had. While she worked at the next fifty pounds, Lois got a job with a furniture store in downtown Salt Lake City called RC Willey selling floor covering. She started doing quite well for a beginner, but she had a nagging feeling that something was holding her back. So one day she went to her boss, Mr. Willey himself, to ask his advice. He handed her a book that he dug out of his bottom drawer.

"It's How To Win Friends and Influence People by Dale Carnegie," he told her as he handed it over. "You read this, follow the directions, and if you don't see a difference then I'm a monkey's uncle."

Lois took the book home and read the entire thing over the weekend. She dog-eared pages that resonated with her most and re-read them daily. As she began to implement the pointers from the book, she actually began to see a change in how people responded to her! Not five months passed before RC Willey put Lois in charge of all the floor covering. At around the same time she received her promotion, Lois received something else she had never anticipated—multiple invitations to go out on dates. There were two men at RC Willey also working in sales who seemed to have been taken with Lois Wright. Each asked her out a number of times, but Lois turned the invitations down, as dating colleagues was against company policy. Although she did not take the men up on their offers to go to the movies, to dinner, or to the opera, the simple acknowledgment from the two male suitors gave the once invisible Lois a tremendous boost to the ego. She had never been pursued by one man, let alone two!

Lois stuck to her new lifestyle and before she knew it had the figure of Audrey Hepburn. In the midst of all her great changes, she came across something as she read the morning paper and sipped her coffee, an advertisement about the upcoming Miss Utah pageant. The paper said that a committee was accepting applications for anyone interested in entering a pageant and the finalist would be able to go on to an interviewing process. The winner would represent the state in the Miss Utah contest. The feeling as she read the article was strangely familiar—the same one she got years ago as she read Giggs's ad! Realizing what kind of impact that night had on her, Lois jumped at the opportunity and applied for the contest. About a week after she had submitted her application, a call came from the pageant committee. She had been selected as a finalist to go in for an interview!

When she arrived at her interview, she was a little nervous, but confident. Just one week after her interview, she received a call that congratulated her for being chosen to compete as one of the contestants for the title of Miss Utah!

Lois was elated. The first thing she did was dash to her closet and pull out a dress covered in opaque plastic. As she peeled the plastic off the dress, she held the beautiful lavender gown from her senior prom in front of her. At that point, the dress could have wrapped around her twice. She hurried the old prom dress to her aunt's seamstress who had sewed it the first time and had the dress altered so that it would fit her for the Miss Utah contest.

"It's my lucky charm," she told the seamstress as she stood praying that a stray pin wouldn't end up in a tender spot on her body.

The competition was held at the Salt Palace in downtown Salt Lake City. When it came down to the final selection, it was Lois's answer that won her the crown. A judge asked, "If you could have dinner with one person, living or deceased, who would it be and why?"

"My mother," Lois answered with misty eyes. "Because she was the most kindhearted woman that walked the earth and because I would like to show her how far I have come in life. I know that she was not president or a famous inventor or poet," she said, "but there is nothing so important as family. Besides that, I believe that most people we fantasize about meeting, they will disappoint us, but I know my mother would not. That is why I would choose her."

Lois left that evening with a bouquet of flowers and a 24-karat crown sitting atop her dark locks of hair.

Here She Comes…

Six months after she was named Miss Utah, Lois went on to Atlantic City and competed against forty-nine other states for the Miss America title. One by one, she worked through each of the events. Again, she would wear her lucky lavender gown for the evening wear section. When it came to the question and answer section, Lois did not disappoint, just as before.

"What are your feelings on education?" a stern-faced judge asked.

"I believe that education, especially for women, is one of the most important things we could have. Education, unlike everything else in the world, can never be taken from us."

Those were the words her mother had said to her just before she died, and as she recited them on stage, she realized how very wise her mother was.

That night the pageant announcer told all of America that that 1942 Miss America was Miss Utah. The year Lois brought the crown to Utah was one of the most joyous years of her life. She traveled around the country and the globe, sporting her sash and the gorgeous crown representing the United States in various parades, speaking events, charity events, social events, and schools. Lois also did some modeling work that year, but the most exciting perk to her crown was a $75,000 scholarship to any university of her choice.

"This is for you, Mama," Lois said as she sent in her application to the University of Utah, and was accepted. Lois studied accounting and became a certified public accountant. Once she graduated, she started working for one of the biggest firms in Utah, where in just three years she became the top accountant. She eventually branched out on her own and started her own accounting firm—she was the only woman in Utah who was a CEO and the owner of a successful accounting firm. Lois kept a picture of her mother on her desk her entire journey to the top.

Dancing Forever

One afternoon Lois got a phone call from a very unlikely individual looking for a good accountant. It was Tommy Evans, the boy she danced with at prom. He was a dentist with his own practice and was interested in Lois's firm, he told her. Lois set up a meeting the following day and before the consultation was complete, Tommy asked her out for their first date. One year later, he got down on one knee and asked Lois to be his wife.

"Yes!" she exclaimed in the middle of a crowded restaurant. "Of course, yes! I have always wished that someday we could dance again."

"We will dance forever," Tommy said and then kissed her on the cheek, just like he did at prom that night. "And I have thought of you since that night too."

Lois married Tommy the following summer. A year later they had their first child, a boy named Thomas Jr. Two years after Thomas was born, the family welcomed Maria. Although Lois had built a successful firm, she opted to step out of her CEO role to raise her beautiful family.

Happily Ever After

"Thomas and I are still married today, and I love him like I did the day he asked me to dance," Lois beamed.

"Now that is something!" Beverly exclaimed.

"It is," Lois agreed.

"Did you ever go back to accounting?" Jeanne asked.

"I dabble a bit," Lois answered. "I never went back full time. I still kept ownership of my firm, so I drop in and I will do a consult or help on a difficult case every now and again, but for the most part I just enjoy life and play a lot of golf."

"So how are the kids then?" Faye asked.

"Oh, they are amazing. Thomas Jr. is now a dentist himself and Maria is a lawyer. We are both so proud of what our family has accomplished."

"It sounds like you have it all, Lois," Faye said.

"All but grandbabies," she sighed. "We just hope the two can take a break from their careers to settle down and give us grandbabies."

"Who would have thought you'd end up with Thomas Evans?" Beverly said, shaking her head. "I'd just have assumed he was shallow like the rest of them. Goes to show you can't judge a book, either way."

"You sure can't," Lois said. "Tommy has been such a blessing. He was always so hard working, but also dedicated to the family. He puts his family first. It was always me and the kids he wanted to be with—none of these drinking buddies like some men."

"He's a keeper," Faye told her.

"He certainly is," Lois said as she nodded.

"So you golf and what else?" Jeanne asked.

"We do a lot of traveling now that Tommy takes fewer patients on. We travel as much as we can. It is amazing to see the world."

"What's been the most intriguing place you've been?" Faye asked.

"China really touched my heart the most, I think," Lois answered. "Only one percent finishes college. Most kids, if they are lucky, get to sixth grade."

"I'd never have guessed that," Faye said. "That's a shame."

"So where's the best place to go?" Faye asked.

"If you want to see the world, save your money and visit the Philippines. The Manila part is the summary of progress, but if you want to see poverty, there is plenty of that all over too."

"We may just have to do that as a group some time," Faye suggested.

"I would love to travel with this fine group of people," Beverly added.

"And so would I," Lois said thoughtfully. "It was this group that helped me change my life, and this man here who put it all together. To Giggs!" Lois said as she held up her nearly empty water glass.

"To Giggs!" the table repeated.

7

The Man of the Hour

"Well, Giggs, we've all been going on and on about what we've been up to, but you haven't told us a word about yourself," Beverly said after she polished off her mimosa. "You're the whole reason we're here and you haven't gotten a word in edgewise over all of us."

"I won't complain for a second," Giggs said as he straightened his spine and sat up a little taller in his chair. "I have had quite a time just taking it all in."

"The fun is over, Gerald," Jeanne announced with a wink. "Now it is your turn to take the hot seat."

"That's right, Giggs," Faye said. "Dish!"

"Well, let's see. It's been a while—a long while," Giggs said with a little chuckle.

"You're making us feel old, Giggs," Faye said shaking her head. "Now you know better than to make a table full of vibrant, young ladies feel old."

"I wouldn't dream of it," Giggs replied. "So where was I?"

"You were stalling," Jeanne said.

"Okay then. Well, after we finished school I joined the Army. I'd like to say it was because I was such a patriot, because I do consider myself a patriot to some degree, but the reason I signed my life away to Uncle Sam was so I could get the GI Bill once I finished in the services to pay for college."

"I don't blame you a bit," Rosela said. "I think it was a very wise thing to do."

Gerald looked at Rosela and smiled a kind of smile that a person reserves for only special people in his life. Rosela noticed the implications behind the curl of Giggs's lips and felt her face flush. Lois nudged Beverly under the table and the two exchanged a furtive glance and a wink.

"After I got out of the Army, I went to college at the University of Utah. I made some decent connections and I also met a beautiful, young woman named June, who I went on to marry and have four children with, a boy and three daughters, who taught me more about life than the Army and college combined. You all probably noticed at the reunion that I went alone." The table nodded and Giggs cleared his throat. "That is because June passed almost five years ago—a car accident," he said. "She was actually driving to see one of our girls, Polly. She had just had our fifth grandchild. June was going to stay with her, but she never made it."

"I'm so sorry, Gerald," Lois whispered as she put a hand on Gerald's.

"I'm okay now," he said. "It was hard—the hardest thing I ever had to go through, but time slowly brought peace, and I trust that June is in a place much better than this one—or I like to think that."

"I'm sure she is," Rosela said.

"June and I had a beautiful life full of beautiful memories, so I'm glad for that. I was able to accomplish a lot with her by my side. We married the minute I graduated from college and I went into residential and commercial development."

"Any neat projects we may have heard of?" Jeanne asked.

"I did a lot of hum-drum stuff when I started, but I eventually started my own firm and our first major undertaking was the Cottonwood Tennis Club. It was a beautiful facility surrounded by elegant home sites and timeshare units."

"That sounds wonderful," Rosela said with adoration in her eyes as she stared at Giggs.

"It really was," Giggs replied. "It really got rolling when the University of Utah tennis team used the courts as their home court. That really put us on the map."

"I bet it did!" Jeanne exclaimed. "That is quite an achievement!"

"It sure was. We made a name for ourselves and compiled a very decent client list. We did quite a few developments that I was more than proud to stamp my name on, but my greatest achievement by far was the Jeramy Ranch Golf and

Country Club. That place I made to feel like nothing short of paradise. I worked side by side with Arnold Palmer to design it. It's still a thriving facility today as a matter of fact."

"So Rosela isn't the only one who rubbed elbows with the stars then," Lois said with a little grin.

"You're one to talk, Miss America!" Faye joked.

"Is that the only famous person you got to work with, Gerald?" Jeanne asked.

"Well, not really," he replied. "I was able to hire enough top-notch people that I could work fewer hours at the firm and started dabbling in other ventures. I'd always been an avid basketball fan, so I decided to buy in on part ownership of the Utah Jazz. This was when Sam Battastone needed a partner with some financial holdings to make the bank happy. He needed a partner and I needed a new business venture, so I figured it was written in the stars."

"Well, Gerald Bagley!" Beverly cried out. "How did I not know you owned the Utah Jazz?"

"Used to." Giggs corrected her. "When the economic disaster happened and everything took a turn for the worse in 1975 things started to look pretty bleak for old Giggs. One by one, all of my projects went belly up, and they were all financed by borrowed money."

"That's awful," Jeanne gasped.

"It certainly was. I ended up losing it all. I went bankrupt. June and I went from living the life to flat broke. Then I lost her on top of it."

"Well, my word, Gerald," Beverly uttered with a shake of the head. "You've had a hell of a stretch."

"I sure have. We had to sell everything. I don't even own my own house now. We had to move to a little rental back near where I grew up. I guess I came around full circle," Giggs said with a sad smile.

"Sometimes we learn some pretty hard lessons," Rosela said. "But learning is the important part."

"I know I learned a real good lesson," Giggs replied. "Everything that happened to me came about from me borrowing money and hoping that things would just continue to fall into place for me. I never thought about the possibility of the economy tanking, or anything really. I just borrowed and built, and borrowed some more. I had an empire built on other folk's money, which I found out is no empire at all. It was just an illusion. And I was left with virtually nothing when the illusion was shattered. Guess my story is pretty pathetic."

"I don't think it is one bit," Rosela said.

"That means more to me than you could ever know," Giggs replied.

"I mean that. You are a good man. That is what makes one successful."

"I hope you mean that," Giggs said.

"I would not say it if I didn't."

"Well, there has been something that I would like to ask you," Giggs said as he rose from his chair.

"What in the world is going on?" Beverly blurted out as she watched Giggs get down on one knee beside Rosela.

"I know I have nothing to offer you but my love, Rosie, but I promise that will never run out."

"Are we on some hidden camera show?" Faye asked, looking around the room.

"We aren't," Giggs said, looking up at Faye. "We haven't said anything, but Rosela and I have been seeing each other for a few months. We didn't want to let the world know yet because we didn't know where it was headed, but I am certain I know where it is going now—or at least where I'd like it to go."

"Oh my," Rosela whispered under her breath as she fanned herself with a hand.

"So, Rosie," Giggs said returning his gaze to her. "Would you have a washed-up nobody like myself as your husband? Will you marry me?"

"Of course I will!" Rosela exclaimed as she wrapped her arms around Giggs's neck.

"Well, isn't this something!" Beverly slapped the table with two palms.

"Now I am glad I didn't pass this up," Jeanne added with a grin.

"Looks like Giggs may get a second shot after all," Faye said to Lois as the table fixed their eyes on the newly engaged couple. "Rosela did just the opposite with the money she made making music. She'll be able to get old Giggs back on his feet. Maybe he could give it another go."

"Maybe," Lois answered. "Maybe."

"I hope you didn't buy that ring on credit, Giggs," Faye joked as Giggs pulled a small, velvety box from his coat jacket.

"I did not," he answered with a grin. "Rosie has taught me a lot already. And I reckon she'll teach me a lot more."

"I reckon I will," Rosela said with a smile.

Author's Other Works

This book is one of the five books written by Dr. Melvin J. Bagley in the last five years. His first book is *Son of a Gun*, a cowboy story about a young kid who is fast with a gun and ends up in a shootout with a gun slinger while protecting his mother.

Dr. Bagley's second book is *Old Bones*, a murder mystery about a school teacher who takes one year out of teaching to go back to school in an attempt to crack a case that the Michigan State Police cannot solve.

The third book is *Celerity Sighting*, a collection of letters accompanying the many pairs of glasses sent to Dr. Melvin J. Bagley to be displayed in The Famous People's Eyeglasses Museum.

The fourth book is *Fight Back*, a story about a mother who teaches her young son who is being bullied in school to fight back. By the end of the tale, the young son teaches his mother the same lesson when he shows her that she too has been bullied by her husband.

The fifth book is *Giggs,* a story about a guy who takes five unpopular girls to prom and changes their lives in amazing ways. The protagonist becomes fabulously rich but does it all on borrowed money, eventually losses everything.

Any of these books can be purchased at Amazon.com or any bookstore. Any profits to be derived from any of the sell from the books will be donated to the Primary Children Hospital in Salt Lake City, Utah.